MY BROTHER IS A ZOMBIE CHILD

by
JONATHAN HARRIS

1
Cheap Manual Labour

Archibald Quinn had heard some strange things in his fifteen years as an Adoption Officer, but this was a new one on him.

'Let me get this straight,' said Quinn. He pushed his glasses up the bridge of his nose, covering his smirk with his hand.

'You already have one child, who you describe as, "not much use around the house", and now you want a "big strong boy" who you think could be useful in "landscaping the garden". However, you "don't like the hassle" that comes with a baby, so you've decided to adopt. In other words, you want us to assign you a child, so you can exploit them for cheap manual labour? Is that correct, Mr Cribbens?'

'Sounds about right, I'd say!' said Joshua Cribbens, flashing a toothy grin. 'Sign the paperwork and we'll be on our way!'

Joshua Cribbens was a rather unfortunate looking man. He was tall and skinny, with thin spindly limbs, and a very large head that was as smooth and round as a bowling ball. Quinn stared at him and wondered how he kept himself upright.

'Oh yes. Please let's get on with it,' interjected Mr Cribbens' wife, Imelda. Imelda was a glamorous blonde who'd been a model at one time and looked a misma

1

with the scrawny Joshua. Today she'd come dressed for the occasion and was head to toe in pink leopard-print. *You never see them that colour in the wild*, thought Quinn.

Imelda continued, 'We need a big, strong boy who can help with the heavy lifting. And they need to be a bit rough, so they can toughen little Ralph up. He's, err, you know, well… weak. And pathetic. Yes, he's weak and pathetic,' she said with a smile, like this was a normal way for a mother to describe her only child.

She couldn't have noticed the smirk on Quinn's face, as she carried on, pressing her point further.

'One with chubby cheeks would be good,' she continued, puckering her lips and making a pinching gesture with her forefinger and thumb. This was, of course, the internationally recognised gesture for chubby cheeks. She had a thing about chubby boys and desired one, in the same way a 9-year-old girl might desire a kitten.

'Right,' said Quinn. He adjusted his spectacles again. 'The thing is, we tend not to be in favour of child slavery. In fact, we're rather strict about it. I'm afraid I cannot possibly recommend you as potential foster parents.'

'But, I don't understand,' insisted Mr Cribbens, his grin turning down ever so slightly at the corners of his mouth. 'Your poster said: *Can you spare a bed for a needy child?* We have a lovely bed up in the attic; it would be just the thing.'

'Mr Cribbens, you said on your form that your own son, Ralph, sleeps in your attic bedroom. What will you do with him when the new child arrives?'

'He can sleep on the sofa until we finish the garden and then he can bed down in the summerhouse!' exclaimed Mr Cribbens, sensing he might be onto something. 'Or they can share. Two boys together up amongst the rafters, what could be more fun?'

'Yes, and Ralph could learn a thing or two from a boy with a decent work ethic!' added Mrs Cribbens. 'He just sits around reading comics all day. What use is he?'

'Why does a child need to have a use?' said Quinn, who was getting irritated. 'Your ideas about adoption are rather inappropriate, and you seem to have a total disregard for your own son's well-being. You would make *terrible* parents for any child we have on our books.'

'No, no, no,' said Mrs Cribbens, bursting into tears that smeared her pink eyeliner. 'My chubby boy! There must be some mistake!' she spun on her husband with her eyes blazing. 'Joshua! Tell him!'

'My wife is quite right,' said Mr Cribbens, putting his long, skinny arms around her. 'We can get a man in to do the garden. And we can put bunk beds in the attic for the boys. Please, just give us a chance!'

'I'm afraid that's not possible.' replied Quinn. 'I've made my mind up and you don't meet the criteria.'

Archibald Quinn pulled a large rubber stamp from his desk, firmly pressed it into a tray of red ink, and brought it crashing down onto the Cribbens application form with a dramatic thump. Sometimes he loved his job.

APPLICATION REJECTED.

'Now good day to you both.'

* * *

3

In the newsagents around the corner from the Adoption Office, Ralph Cribbens kneeled behind the sweet section, flicking through a comic. Ralph was trying to keep a low profile. The proprietor of the newsagent, Mr Ronnie Rosebud, knew Ralph well and considered him a "persona non grata". A person unwelcome in Mr Rosebud's establishment. Mr Rosebud had identified Ralph as someone who was always loitering around his shop reading comics for which he had not paid and never would. Mr Rosebud had seen him enough times, working his way through the comic-book shelf, covering the comics with his greasy fingerprints and getting the edges all tatty so that no paying customer would even consider buying them. Whenever Mr Rosebud spotted Ralph lurking in his shop, he would pick up his broom and rustle Ralph out through the door, pushing him with the bristly end as if sweeping out an enormous crisp packet blown in by the wind.

Ralph was well aware of Mr Rosebud's opinion of him, and he didn't disagree with it. In fact, it was a dream of his to one day run his own comic book store and should that dream ever come to pass, Ralph intended to display his own comic books in cellophane sheaths to discourage any unwanted thumbing. Nor would Ralph have read his comics in this fashion had he any other choice. He loved comics; he had done ever since he'd first picked up a discarded copy of *Spiderman* in the doctor's waiting room, and he felt compelled to read them. To consume them, in fact. He loved everything about them, even the smell. He always thought they should taste delicious too, but he'd tried a few times and they didn't live up to expectations on that front.

4

Unfortunately for Ralph, his father, Joshua Cribbens, did not share Ralph's passion for comics. He never gave Ralph pocket money anyway, but even if he had done so, he regarded comics as "pointless fantasy" and would never have agreed to Ralph wasting money on them. So Ralph's adventures between the pages became an illicit pursuit; something secret. He read his comics at night by torchlight huddled under his duvet. He had a few comics that he'd picked up here and there, and he kept them stashed in his room in an old sea chest that he'd found between the beams of his attic bedroom.

Ralph's lived at number 1, Bushy Lane, in the town of Great Merritt, which was slap-bang in the middle of what Ralph thought must be the least interesting part of England. The most remarkable thing about Great Merritt was that, despite its name, it was a place of very little merit. This contrasted with the nearby village of Little Merritt, which had been named Britain's Neatest Village on no less than four separate occasions.

Number 1, Bushy Lane was a rather small house with only one bedroom. There was a small box room, but Ralph's Mother had set up a home gym in there with a rowing machine and a skiing simulator. Ralph slept in the attic on a rickety old iron bedstead. Ralph's parents had not bothered to move the old junk out of the attic when they moved him in, so Ralph lived amongst the piles of old bric-à-brac and dusty books.

There were no floorboards throughout most of the room. His parents considered these an 'unnecessary expense'. They didn't need lighting either, as the Cribbens's "didn't go up there much".

More than once, Ralph had almost come crashing down through the ceiling when he'd lost his footing while working his way through the criss-cross of beams. It was on one of these occasions, while on his way for a late-night visit to the bathroom, when he'd found the battered old sea chest. He'd lost his footing and caught himself on the beams just in time to stop himself falling through the plaster into his parent's bedroom below. When he looked up he'd spotted the chest in front of him. It had been under the eaves so he'd never noticed it before, but it was the perfect place to stash his comics. Especially as his parents rarely made the effort to climb the ladder to his room.

It was difficult to lose yourself in the story when you were reading in the newsagent. That was the trouble. Ralph needed to remain on high alert for Mr Rosebud's traditional bellow of "this is not a library!". If he didn't, he'd come back to reality with a bump when he felt the spiny bristles of Mr Rosebud's brush scratching at his face.

When he was in his attic bedroom, the stories would transport him to another world where life was less dull. Where Ralph, instead of being a pathetic nobody with embarrassingly weird parents, could put himself into the shoes of a superhero or a vampire hunter.

On this occasion, though, Ralph was glad that he had his wits about him. He'd just got to a bit in the story where the hero had found out that the British Prime Minister was a secret werewolf, when he noticed somebody looming over him.

'What are you reading there, Cribbens?' Ralph's heart sank. He recognized the gravelly voice as belonging to

Breezeblock. If there was someone you didn't want to find you squatting in a shop reading comics, it was Breezeblock. Despite being Ralph's age, he was bigger than most men and wasn't afraid to throw his weight around with the other kids. As usual Breezebock was with his two hangers-on, a short girl with a sharp mouth called Parsnip and a large rotund boy called Plomp. They liked to call themselves the "Wrecking Crew" and would scrawl the name of their gang on bathroom stalls and benches around the town.

'Didn't know you could read Cribbens,' said Parsnip. 'I'm actually quite impressed. Though that is exactly the sort of weirdo magazine I'd expect you to like.'

'He's probably just looking at the pictures Parsnip,' said Breezeblock, snatching the comic out of Ralph's hands. 'Look at it, it's a picture book for thick kids who never learned their alphabet.'

Bit of a cheek coming from you three, thought Ralph. They were rarely at school. When they were, all they did was mess around, winding up the teachers or intimidating kids out of their lunch money.

'I err, I'm not reading it, I'm just waiting for my Dad so, um, I just popped in here.' Ralph felt embarrassed telling other kids he was into comics. They weren't cool, and he didn't like feeling judged. The only one who knew about his obsessions was his friend Sunny. Despite her many other failings, she would never judge him for anything like that. 'Just passing the time,' he added.

'Did you say you're with your Dad? Old pipe-cleaner legs is about, is he? Trust the weirdest teacher in the school to have the weirdest kid. What's he doing then?'

Ralph had no intention of bringing the whole adoption situation into the discussion. 'He's um, getting his hair cut,' lied Ralph.

'Haha where at?' guffawed Parsnip. 'Surely it's not worth paying someone to cut that? I always thought he just popped his head in the ball polisher at the bowling alley!'

Parsnip's comment caused guffaws of laughter, but when the chuckles died down, Breezeblock's face turned serious. 'Anyway Cribben's, nice as it is to chat, we came over to see you for a reason. You see, we were just passing the shop when Plomp here,' he clapped Plomp on the shoulder, 'Plomp's belly started rumbling and we realised all of a sudden that it's coming up for lunchtime. Only problem is that we've all forgot to bring our lunch money. There we were, thinking we'd have to go hungry. But, out of the corner of her eye, Parsnip spots you through the window of the shop. "There's our friend Cribbens!" we all say, "he'll look after us", so we were wondering Cribbens, if you could, maybe, buy us all a chocolate bar?'

'Two for me,' added Plomp.

'Well, I would do obviously,' said Ralph, nervously standing up and popping the comic back on its rack. 'Only I don't have any money so I—'

Parsnip leaned right into his face, close enough that he could see the thick make-up that she'd stolen from her mum to plaster over her spots. 'Come on, Cribbens, if you have no money, how were you going to buy your weird magazine?'

'I was just browsing, I wasn—'

'That's fine, Cribbens.' Breezeblock put a patronly arm around him. 'If you don't have money, don't worry about it.'

Ralph breathed out a sigh of relief. These three could be a bit menacing sometimes, but he supposed they weren't too bad, deep down. 'Okay,' he said.

Breezeblock gave Ralph a warm smile. 'All you need to do is pop a few bars into your pocket and slip out of the door while we keep old Rosebud busy.'

Ralph's jaw dropped open. They couldn't seriously be asking him to steal the chocolate, could they?

'Then just nip around the corner. We'll meet you there in a minute.' Plomp patted Ralph on the shoulder with a heavy hand, smiling as if this was all normal behavior between friends.

'What you mean—'

'It's just a couple of chocolate bars Cribbens,' said Parsnip. 'Rosebud won't even miss them.'

'But I need to meet my Dad.'

'That's fine Cribben's, just pop the bars in your pocket now and we can get going,' said Breezeblock in a pleasant tone, though his face twisted with a nasty smile. 'You won't be late for your Dad.'

'Well I err, I guess I,' Ralph swayed back trying to put some breathing space in between himself and Breezeblock. He could feel himself getting flushed. As he leaned away, his shoulder bumped against the rack of cheap pocket money toys and sent it clattering to the ground, spilling toys all over the floor.

Mr Rosebud looked up from the newspaper he was reading, saw his carefully displayed plastic tat lying scattered across his shop floor, and stormed over to the kids in a rage. 'Ralph Cribbens, is that you? I've told you before to keep out of my shop, this isn't a library you know! And you've brought your friends with you this time I see.' He eyeballed Breezeblock who just raised an eyebrow and smirked back. 'I suppose word must have got around that you can read comics for free at Ronnie Rosebud's, eh? And now you've crammed in here and ruined my display. Get out! The lot of you!'

'Sorry Mr Rosebud,' said Parsnip, 'It was Cribbens, like you said. He made out you and him were friends. But it's obvious now that he was lying.'

'On your way, you three,' Rosebud opened the door and turned back to Ralph, 'Cribbens, you can help me pick this up before you go or I'll be speaking to your father. And after this, I don't want to see you in my shop again. Not unless you are waving a ten pound note as you walk in. Do I make myself clear?'

Ralph nodded his head as Breezeblock, Parsnip, and Plomp sloped out of the shop. Helping Mr Rosebud tidy up would let *The Wrecking Crew* get a head start; he didn't want them seeing him meet Dad outside the Adoption Office.

As he picked up a pair of plastic police handcuffs and hung them on the rack, he eyed the comic he'd been reading and wondered if he could sneak another look before he left and Mr Rosebud banned him for good.

* * *

'It's outrageous,' said Mr Cribbens as they drove home from the adoption office. 'How can that man get away with it? It's a national disgrace! Children starving on our streets and he thinks he can turn us away. Our charity is not good enough. Well, he won't stop me. No siree Bob.'

'Oh Joshua,' sighed Mrs Cribbens. 'It's over. Why don't we just leave it now?'

'Leave it?' replied Mr Cribbens, his mouth tightening into a line of shock and disgust.

'Can you believe this, Ralph? Imelda wants to leave it! She wants to abandon your brother.'

'I don't have a brother.' argued Ralph without thinking.

The car careered across the road, instigating a torrent of angry beeping from other vehicles as Mr Cribbens turned around to address his son directly.

'Don't be so selfish!' he snapped, focusing his anger on Ralph like a prison spotlight on a fleeing convict. 'You do have a brother, you just haven't met him yet! We've been through this Ralph. I expect you to treat him like you've known him all his life when he arrives. That means a big hug as soon as he walks through the door, like you would with any relative.'

Ralph decided not to bring up the fact that he didn't do hugs and had hugged no one since he was six-years-old. Sunny Brightwell had hugged him, but it was different if it wasn't reciprocated.

'But Joshua,' said Imelda. 'It's impossible. They'll never change their mind now! Not after you called Mr Quinn a "baboon in a man suit," and drew a beard on that picture of his wife.'

'The beard was already there,' retorted Mr Cribbens. 'I was merely highlighting her substandard shaving regime. But don't you worry, Imelda, we'll get our boy. I have a plan.'

2
House of Strife

'Blast these do-gooding celebrities!' exclaimed Joshua Cribbens as he turned away in disgust from the computer. 'The price of orphans is through the roof since it's become fashionable to adopt a needy child! I don't think we'll be able to afford one after all, Imelda.'

After watching a programme on the television about famous people who adopted children from other countries, Joshua had decided that he and Imelda could do the same. It was the perfect way to get around the utterly unreasonable behaviour of the British adoption services. He'd scoured the internet looking for someone who could provide him with a child. He wasn't too bothered about where they came from as long as they were within budget. Unfortunately, adopting a child from outside your own country involves permits, background checks, travel arrangements for visits back and forth, and a whole host of other fees. All in all, it can be rather an expensive process when done via the official channels.

'Oh no!' wailed his wife. 'The dream is over… will we never see our darling boy?' she sighed and let her head drop 'Perhaps it's just not meant to be. We have Ralphie, after all. Even if he isn't much use.'

'I am here, you know,' Ralph cut in. Ralph was used to being ignored by his parents, and it rarely bothered him. Since this adoption thing had begun, though, it had annoyed him more and more. It was like they wanted to adopt because he didn't cut the mustard and they wanted a replacement son.

'Imelda knows that Ralph,' said his dad. Imelda allowed neither Ralph nor her husband to refer to her as 'Mum'. Maybe being called 'Mum' made her feel old. Maybe she just didn't want anyone to realise Ralph was her son. Ralph didn't know, but she was always Imelda to him.

'It does you good to hear a few home truths from time to time,' Dad continued, 'it's character building. And if…' Joshua Cribbens trailed off from the inevitable rant as something on the monitor caught his eye.

'Hold on a minute. What's this? *Dr Romeronov's House of Strife - For kids who need a second life.*' The picture on the screen showed a sad faced child staring blankly from the window of a rickety old orphanage.

'We could help them!' cried Imelda, leaping into the air in excitement. 'We could give them a second life!'

Ralph rolled his eyes.

'Calm yourself, Imelda!' said Mr Cribbens, barely able to contain his own excitement. 'We don't know the prices yet. Let's just have a look.'

Mr Cribbens took hold of the mouse and clicked the link to the orphanage. After what seemed an eternity of painful loading, the webpage flashed up on screen. It didn't appear to be the most inviting of websites. The page was black with red text and a single faded sepia photograph of a crumbling old building that Ralph supposed housed the orphans; the photograph looked like it dated back to the 1920s. The long wooden building resembled the prisoner of war camps that Ralph had seen in history class at school. Just looking at the building gave Ralph the creeps. Ralph thought he could even see a barbed wire fence at the edge of the photograph. *What an awful place to grow up*, he thought. It made him feel thankful for the small comforts of his attic room.

Mr Cribbens had located the 'Browse Orphans' button and was now loading a page with a selection of the latest orphans to become available for adoption. The screen filled with images of bedraggled looking children staring into the camera. Ralph guessed they were all desperate to get adopted, but the way their eyes followed him made him feel a little uncomfortable.

'They all look very skinny,' said Mrs Cribbens, sounding dubious.

'But the price is right!' Mr Cribbens scrolled through the first page of children. 'Looks like we're in before the celebs! And I'm sure we could feed them up. What about this one?' he said, pointing to a scrawny boy with yellow, strawlike hair.

'Too pale.'

'How about this one here?' said her husband, showing her a tall boy with teeth jutting from his mouth at awkward angles.

'Too tall,' sighed Mrs Cribbens.

Mr Cribbens moved the cursor over a girl with enormous watery eyes and pigtails, 'She could be a good one'.

'Too female.' Mrs Cribbens hung her head.

'Imelda, be reasonable! We can't afford to be choosey.'

'Okay, okay,' said Imelda, moving in for a closer look. 'What about this boy? He doesn't have a lot of meat on him, but he's big boned. I think he might plump up nicely.'

'Yes, I think you're right. He looks ideal. He could be a good, sturdy lad with a couple of your famous meatball dinners inside him.'

'Oh yes, yes! He's the one for us. I'm certain of it. What do you think, Ralphie?' said Imelda.

'Well, his teeth look a little… pointy. I'm sure he's perfectly nice though.' Ralph was far from convinced the boy was 'perfectly nice'. He felt quite the opposite after looking into the cold, staring eyes. He put it down to his own resentment about having an unwanted brother forced upon him; it seemed unfair not to give the boy the benefit of the doubt. He didn't want to enrage his father either, but it seemed he had annoyed him anyway.

'It's not a beauty contest, Ralph,' snapped his father. 'This boy needs our help and all you can do is criticise his appearance! Go to your room if you can't be civil!'

Ralph moped up to his room. When his parents were in this kind of mood, he was happy to get away from them and back to his comic books. At the same time, Ralph felt side-lined by the whole adoption thing. He knew he was very different to his parents, it was unusual if he saw eye-to-eye with them, but he never imagined they would end up wanting to replace him with another child. Especially one who looked so freakish. Something about the boy in the photograph worried Ralph. Some primitive savagery that Ralph couldn't put his finger on.

* * *

Downstairs, Mr Cribbens located the 'buy one now' button. He hovered the mouse over it for a second and clicked it, opening the payment screen. Mr Cribbens selected the 'brilliant-bargain' delivery.

'For goodness' sake, Joshua!' said Imelda. 'Do you always have to be so cheap? If you choose the "super-fast send out" we'll have him here tomorrow.'

'What's the rush? We need to get his room ready. I suppose we should get a bunk-bed after what the adoption agency said. Perhaps I could make one. We'd save a bit of money and it would be a welcoming gesture. I'm sure he'd love it if he knew we'd made the effort to build him a bed.'

'Oh, how lovely,' cooed Mrs Cribbens as Mr Cribbens scribbled down the order number.

* * *

Up in his penthouse retreat - as he imagined an estate agent might describe his cramped attic hovel - Ralph snuggled under his covers with his favourite scary comic, *Dark Secrets*, but he just couldn't concentrate. This whole adoption business had been playing on his mind. He normally had no interest in what his parents were up to; he just ignored their snippy comments and got on with doing his own thing. This was different, though. He knew he frustrated his parents with his laziness around the house and his lack of any interest in their little projects like landscaping the garden, but he'd always assumed that they *kind* of enjoyed having him around. Now it looked like he was being replaced by a newer, more masculine, European wonder son. He was redundant. He considered packing up his stuff and just taking off, but he knew he'd never be able to carry all his beloved comics and didn't think he was cut out for life on the road.

Ralph decided he would wait and see what happened. The new kid could be fun after all, and it wasn't his fault that Ralph's parents had decided to 'adopt' him through a dubious online agency. Ralph wondered if the whole thing was even legal. He guessed not, but reasoned that even though his parents were turned away by the British adoption agency, they weren't *that* bad. He supposed they were doing a good thing; the orphanage had looked like an awfully forbidding place.

Ralph thought about the creepy building those poor orphaned children had to live in. He shivered as he pictured an icy wind blowing through the rotting timber; the orphans huddled together for warmth, their thin pyjamas providing little protection against the biting cold. In Ralph's mind, packs of rats plagued the corridors of the orphanage, and bats streamed through the rafters after dark. The images he'd seen online made it difficult to imagine anything else.

Ralph could not concentrate on his comic so he packed it away in his chest before getting back into bed and settling down to sleep.

Ralph's eyes grew heavy and his head filled with dark dreams of vampires and werebeasts.

As he dozed, Ralph noticed a flinty tapping sound, 'tap… tap… tap'. Something was clambering towards him across the attic beams. Ralph didn't dare to turn his head, but he knew it was something horrible, a skeleton, its bony feet clacking against the wood. He heard it call his name as it moved closer, its fleshless jaw crunching out the words.

'Raaaalph, Raaaalph!' it called, sounding as if it was chewing a mouthful of marbles. 'Raaaalph!'

The skeleton was on him, its fingers closing around his throat. Ralph thrashed around, struggling for breath. He kicked out of his bad and staggered to his feet, ready to run.

He looked around, surprised to find himself alone in the familiar surroundings of his attic. There was no sign of the skeleton, it had vanished. Still unsure if he was dreaming, Ralph held his breath while he double checked if there was anything to worry about. It seemed the coast was clear, so he allowed himself to breathe and gave an involuntary chuckle. *Just a bad dream.* It was rare that he suffered from nightmares and rarer still that they affected him once he'd woken up, but he put it down to the overwhelming day he'd had and the weird staring eyes of the creepy orphan.

He crawled back under his covers.

tap-tap-tap!

Ralph leaped from his bed like he was being electrocuted. He couldn't see the skeleton, but it could be anywhere in the untidy attic. Right on top of him, even. He wouldn't know until it was too late.

'Raaaalph!' it called, though its voice had softened and was sounding less like rocks rubbing together.

There was another loud *tap* followed by the sound of breaking glass, as the skylight behind him cracked.

3
A Most Unusual Package

'Oops! Sorry Ralphie!'

This wasn't the first time Sunny Brightwell had featured in one of Ralph's nightmares, though usually she was trying to kiss him rather than eat him.

'Sunny! Look what you've done. Dad is going to go ape if he finds out!' Ralph moved to the window and peered at the female figure below him in the darkness. 'I'll have to patch it with some cling film to stop the wind blowing into my bedroom.'

'Are you in bed already?' shouted the girl. 'Let me in!'

Ralph opened the window. A second later he could hear a pop and whirring noise before a grappling hook looped into his bedroom and gripped onto his window ledge. A moment later Sunny's curly blonde hair appeared over the sill and she pulled herself up over the ledge and dropped into the room with a dramatic, 'tada!'

'Yes, I've seen that little trick before,' yawned Ralph.

'It never gets old though, does it?' said Sunny with a grin. 'I think I've perfected the pulley mechanism now. Did you see how fast I whizzed up here?'

As much as Sunny annoyed Ralph with her endless chirpiness, foghorn voice and constant declarations of love for him, he admired her skill with any sort of gadgetry. The grappling hook launcher that allowed her to fire a hook just about anywhere and use its electric motors to pull her along after it was just one of her many ingenious inventions. To Ralph she was both intelligent and irritating; what Ralph liked to think of as

19

"intelli-tating" and was already studying for her GCSEs in Maths, Chemistry and Physics. She was also his dad's star pupil in the Design and Technology class he taught at school.

'Yes, well, rather you than me, I'm not sure I'd trust my life to that thing,' said Ralph. 'Can I help you with something? Why are you out at this time of night, anyway?'

'Ha! I go out when I like. Do you really think my simple-minded parents can contain me?'

'Well, no, I suppose not Sunny, but you're not in the habit of creeping around the streets at night, are you?'

'Usually not, I guess…' agreed Sunny, her eyes twinkling with conspiratorial glee. 'OK, I'll tell you what I'm doing out. You know old Mr Binns who lives over on Winterbrook Lane?'

Ralph nodded and rolled his eyes. He sat back down on the bed expecting this to go on for a while. Sunny's stories rarely made much sense.

'Earlier on I was testing my new cyber-scope binoculars and guess who I saw him with….'

'So you were spying on him. I see. Carry on.'

'I was not spying on him. I only do that to you,' she said, giving him a cheeky wink. 'Go on, take a guess.'

'The Easter Bunny.'

'Its October, walnut-brain! Would the Easter Bunny be around in October?'

'Good point,' Ralph gave a serious nod. 'I don't know what I was thinking.'

'Exactly. Anyway, as I was saying, I saw old Binnsy all alone in his back garden…'

'Hold on,' Ralph cut in. 'You asked me to guess who you saw him with, didn't you?'

'That's right. Try to keep up.' Sunny continued.

'But then you said he was on his own in his garden.'

'Yes Ralph, that's my point. Mr Binns is *never* alone, is he? He's always with his weird wife. You know, the one that tries to prod you with her walking stick if you get too close and smells of pickled onions?'

'Ok, so what is your point?' said Ralph, failing to see the point.

'Well, isn't it obvious? He's murdered her! He's buried the body in the back garden.'

'What? So… he was digging a hole when you saw him?' said Ralph, taken aback at the thought of a murderer on the loose in Great Merritt.

'He was pruning his privet hedge.' Sunny admitted. 'But you should've seen the way he was wielding his shears. He was like a man possessed!'

'Riiiiight,' said Ralph with a huff. 'You're accusing a man of bumping off his wife purely because she isn't home and he's gardening a *little* too enthusiastically.'

Sunny hesitated. 'Well… when you put it like that… it does sound a little far-fetched but Ralphie, I'm telling you it's fishy. They're joined at the hip. And I've never known him to do gardening. Don't you think it's a little late to start at his age?'

'She'll just be visiting that sister of hers in Scotland or something.' said Ralph.

Sunny pursed her lips, then sighed and nodded with a resigned look. 'I suppose you're right. I just thought something interesting might happen in this boring old town for once.'

Ralph nodded in agreement, but then he remembered the adoption.

'Actually,' he said. 'I haven't told you about my new brother yet.'

'Your new brother?' said Sunny, confused. 'But Imelda isn't pregnant, is she?'

'No, she's not pregnant. They're adopting… they think I need a brother to toughen me up,' he said with a shrug. 'No idea what he'll be like, but it might make things more interesting around here.'

He looked at Sunny and smiled. 'He's coming all the way from Transylvania.'

'Ooh, now that sounds interesting.' She settled herself down on top of his sea chest and listened as Ralph explained the whole adoption story to her. They didn't know it but things really were about to get interesting. *Dead* interesting.

* * *

'Ah, Ralphie! Have I got a treat for you today?!' cried Ralph's stepmother from the kitchen as Ralph let himself in after another tedious day at school.

'I don't know Imelda, have you?' his sarcasm was lost on her, as it always was on her and Dad.

Ralph could have got a lift back from school with Dad but preferred to walk, as he knew his father would spend the journey ranting about the "talentless blockheads" he had to teach. He'd worried it might rain, but he'd managed to make it back home before the heavens opened.

'Oh yeah, you're going to love this,' Imelda continued, 'I've made some lovely traditional food from Eastern Europe. We'll be eating this all the time when your brother arrives, so I thought I'd better practice some recipes.'

'I guess.' said Ralph, trying not to commit himself until after he'd tasted it.

Imelda Cribbens broke the surface of one of her pans with a wooden spoon, and an overpowering aroma of cabbage wafted from the bubbling liquid. She scooped out a spoonful of green mush and gave it a long, deep sniff.

'Perfect! I think that's ready. Why don't you lay the table Ralphie?'

Gagging on the stink of cabbage, Ralph could not reply, so he mutely set about fetching the knives and forks and laying them around the table.

The back door creaked open and Ralph's dad burst in from the garden.

'What is that wonderful smell Imelda?' he said, joy written all over his face.

'You'll have to wait and see,' she teased. 'Why don't you both sit down, I can see you boys are hungry.'

She shooed them to the table and Ralph and his dad took their seats while Imelda busied herself dishing out the food.

'First up we have some boiled cabbage,' she said, slopping it onto the plates. 'They love their cabbage in Transylvania. I'm told they have it with everything.' Ralph had once had cabbage in a meal from the Chinese takeaway that had been delicious, but whenever Imelda cooked it, somehow it turned into a pile of congealed slop with a horrifying stink. Luckily, she didn't cook it often, or at least she hadn't until now.

'I'm not sure they serve it like this, Imelda,' Ralph tried not to look at the quivering mush on his plate.

'Nonsense. What other way could you serve cabbage?'

Ralph could think of at least three ways off the top of his head, but you couldn't argue with her. His preferred method of serving it would have been directly into the bin.

Imelda opened the door to their old gas oven, bent down and lifted out a large, steaming casserole dish.

What delight do we have here? thought Ralph.

Imelda placed the dish on the table and removed the lid. To Ralph's surprise, the smell that came wafting out was rather good. Onions, garlic, cream and meat. Not much could go wrong with that. Dinner was looking up.

Imelda took a large ladle and began spooning the stew onto the plates. Ralph noticed one ingredient had an unusual texture, almost like honeycomb. 'What's this stuff? Snake?' he joked.

'Hahaha don't be silly, Ralphie. It's not snake. It's tripe.'

'Tripe?' asked Ralph, before filling his mouth with the steaming meat. 'Never heard of it.'

'You know, it's the inside of a cow's stomach. My grandma used to eat it all the time. I don't know why it went out of fashion.' Imelda patted her tummy to emphasise the point.

Ralph's appetite vanished in an instant. His eyes grew wide with shock and the fork he'd been holding clattered to the floor. The mouthful of stew he'd just swallowed churned in his stomach.

Imelda must have noticed the expression on Ralph's face. 'It's very tasty actually,' she said with a sniff. She gave Ralph an angry glare. 'I'm sure our new boy will love it.'

'I'm sure he will too,' agreed Dad. He was trying to be supportive, but Ralph could see him flinch when he tried a mouthful. 'Delicious! If you don't want yours, Ralph, I'll have it. Can't get enough!' He braced himself for a second mouthful.

'Help yourself then.' said Ralph, with a sadistic grin. 'I think I'm going to go up to my room, I've had a busy day at school.'

'OK Ralph, but you need to get more used to trying exotic foods. We'll be eating them all the time soon. Fish fingers are history in this house.'

'Fine,' agreed Ralph through gritted teeth. 'As long as you don't serve up stomach again,' he added under his breath.

* * *

Late that night, as Ralph lay in bed flicking through a comic, it rained. It started as a few light pitter-patters but, after a moment, heavy droplets began to hammer on the roof above him.

The brooding threat of thunder made the air feel heavy and charged. A rickety old truck rattled into Bushy Lane at a speed much too fast for the weather. A speeding truck, a wet road and non-existent visibility did not make for a happy ending, but somehow the truck skidded to a halt right outside Ralph's front door. The driver hopped from his carriage and sprinted to the rear. He jumped up onto the back of the truck, which held a large wooden crate. Giving the crate a quick once over to make sure it was okay, he took a crowbar from his jacket and jammed it underneath the crate. Using it as a lever, he tipped the crate forward, so it toppled off the truck, landing on the tarmac with a crack of splintering timber. Without stopping to check the crate again, he ran to the Cribbens' front door, rang the bell and sprinted back to his cab. Wheels spinning on the slippery road, the truck sped off, even faster than it had arrived.

The door opened a crack and the long nose of Joshua Cribbens appeared as he peeped out, wondering what was going on.

The Cribbens were not late-night people, nor did they have an army of friends and well-wishers regularly knocking on their door, so to be called upon at such an hour was most unexpected. In fact, Joshua Cribbens had been so startled to hear the buzzer that the shock of it caused him to toss the tea he'd been drinking from its cup. It slopped into the air and landed with a warm-wet slap in the middle of his lap, making him even warier about opening the door. If it was someone important, he didn't want to give the impression that he was a man who was not the master of his own bodily functions.

Seeing nobody, Mr Cribbens cautiously opened the door fully to give himself a view of the street. He peered through the wet night, and could just about make out the outline of the crate lying in the road outside his house.

This unusual sight was enough to arouse the interest of even a suspicious man with an unfortunate stain on his lap, so throwing caution to the wind Mr Cribbens dashed into the downpour without even a thought for preserving the dryness of his slippers. He could see the crate was a sturdy one, but it was damaged somehow, like someone had dropped it from a great height. He wondered whether it might have fallen off the back of a lorry. It was his doorbell ringing that had brought him out in the first place though, so this was not something that had dropped here by accident.

Joshua Cribbens noticed a piece of card attached to the crate by a worn and grimy looking piece of string. Picking it up, he could make out that someone had scrawled his own address on it in a spidery hand. Equally poor spelling matched the sender's atrocious handwriting.

Mr J Crribens

1 Bushee Layne

Grate Merrrit

Englund

'What is it Joshua?' shouted Imelda from inside the front door.

'I'm not sure... Hold on. There's a return address on the back of the label,' Mr Cribbens leaned in to get a closer look in the darkness. 'I can't quite make it out, but it looks like it's written in Italian or something...'

'Transylvanian?' Imelda could barely contain her excitement.

'I hardly think they would deliver the boy in the middle of the night,' Mr Cribbens mocked, as he started pulling at the wooden slats that made up the crate sides.

'Whatever it was, there's nothing in here now. Blast that Post Office! The service gets worse every year.'

Before Joshua Cribbens could go any further with his rant about the Post Office, he spotted something else on the top of the crate.

'There's a stamp!'

On closer examination, he could see the picture was of a bleak and forbidding landscape with some lonely-looking mountains rising in the distance. The way they cast their shadow over the surrounding land was almost haunting.

'It's a picturesque view of the Carpathian Mountains! I take it all back, Imelda. It is from Transylvania.'

Imelda smiled, but then her face darkened. 'You and your super saver delivery. They packed the poor little boy in a crate. How could they send a boy in a crate? And now he has gone missing. Gonnnnne! Lost in the wilderness of a new and distant land. Oh the poor, poor child!' she wailed.

A boom of thunder stifled the loudest of her sobs.

Joshua was about to reply when a jagged streak of lightning illuminated the night.

If Joshua had not been looking right at Imelda when it happened he would never have noticed, but shambling towards her from the darkness with his arms outstretched was a pale and emaciated boy.

'Imelda lookout!' shouted Joshua as stabbed a bony finger towards the approaching boy. 'He's coming to hug you!'

Imelda took a sharp intake of breath and turned, hardly able to believe her eyes.

'Oh, my boy! Look at you, soaked to the skin! Come to Mamma,' she reached past his outstretched arms and gathered him up in an embrace. 'Oh my! You are light as a feather. We'll soon fix that! Let's get you inside and get some food in you, shall we?'

Joshua grinned his famous grin, picked up the crate from the road and followed them inside the house.

* * *

Upstairs in the attic, Ralph could hear the commotion from downstairs. He'd just got to a meaty bit in his comic, so he decided whatever it was could wait.

'Ralph! Ralph, come down. We have a surprise for you.'

Ralph rolled his eyes. He supposed he'd better go down. With great care he marked his page with a strip of paper torn from his Maths exercise book, and hurried through the ritual of hiding his comics away. It was something he always did, just in case he couldn't get back before his parents came nosing around. As unlikely as either of them bothering to climb the ladder to the attic was, it was a risk he was unwilling to take. Getting busted with his comics and having them confiscated, was the worst thing Ralph could imagine. They were his sanctuary.

'Come on, Ralphie,' called Imelda. 'Everybody is waiting for you!'

'Who's everybody?' muttered Ralph.

He finished stashing his comics and made his way to the trapdoor in the attic. At the bottom of the stairs, Imelda and dad were waiting for him, along with someone else he recognised. He knew who it was at once, even from the poor-quality photograph he'd seen on the website. It was a face you didn't forget in a hurry.

Pale and ghostlike, the skin covering the face stretched tight across the skull. So tight, in fact, that the lips pulled away from the mouth, as if the skin didn't quite fit. The mouth itself was a hideous thing. Sharp pointed teeth jutted from it at every angle, some of which were yellow, the rest a dark brown like varnished oak.

The boy it belonged to must have been standing outside in the rain for a while. The rain had plastered his black hair to his head and it appeared to drip with a white grease. This did not seem to concern the boy in the slightest. He was thin, gaunt even. He looked like hadn't had a decent meal in months. His clothing resembled something you would see in a history book about the Victorians. A shirt with a waistcoat, short trousers and a flat cap.

The smell coming off him made Ralph gag. it reminded him of the time he and Sunny had found a dead bird in an abandoned shed on the allotments. When they had rolled it over with a stick, maggots had come crawling from underneath. They'd screamed and run away, horrified.

The new boy didn't seem to have any maggots on him, but Ralph was still fighting the urge to scream and run. The worst thing about the newcomer wasn't his looks or his dress sense or even the smell. It was his eyes. They looked like the light behind them had gone out. Ralph became transfixed by them for a moment and felt like he was staring into bottomless black holes. When Ralph tore his eyes away, he noticed the boy was wearing a modern name badge sticker coated in the thick slimy saliva that was drooling from his mouth. It read 'Hello, my name is Luca.'

'Well, don't just stand there Ralph, say hello to your brother!' ordered his dad.

'Hello Luca,' said Ralph.

'Luca? Oh um, actually we were…' his dad dithered. 'We were thinking of giving him a traditional

Transylvanian name. Like, you know, Igor or something. But if you like Luca…'

Ralph's dad looked quizzically at Imelda.

'No, no. I don't want to give him a name, but I think his name is Luca,' Ralph cut in quickly to stave off any embarrassment. 'He's wearing a name badge,' Ralph pointed to the sticker that looked like the ones his dad would sometimes be wearing when he'd come back from a teaching conference or training day. 'So, I'm guessing it's his name.'

'Hahaha of course,' said Imelda. She slapped herself on the forehead and then turned on her husband. 'How on earth did you miss that, Joshua? Of course his name is Luca.' Imelda turned towards Luca. 'Loooooca! My little Luca!' She tried to pinch his cheek and give it a little wiggle but there wasn't enough skin to get a grip so she just patted him on the head, looking a little embarrassed. 'Oh, your skin, it feels so cold!' Turning to Ralph and Joshua she said, 'The poor boy is so cold and hungry. Should we give him food first or a hot shower?'

'Shower,' said Ralph and his dad in unison, both of them thinking less about the poor freezing orphan and more about the astonishing odour he was giving off.

'Yes, you're right, of course. He won't enjoy his food if he is sitting there shivering, the poor little thing.'

In fact, Luca wasn't shivering at all. He didn't seem bothered in the slightest that the ice-cold rainwater had soaked him to the skin. Ralph supposed he was just a product of the unpredictable Transylvanian climate and must spend a lot of time outdoors, digging for turnips or whatever they did over there. Ralph wasn't up-to-date with the ins and outs of the Transylvanian economy, but in his mind it was quite agricultural.

'Ralph, why don't you show Luca where the bathroom is?' said Imelda. 'While he's in the shower could you bring down some old clothes for him too?'

Great, thought Ralph. *First, he moves into my room and now he wants to wear my clothes. What's next? Stealing my identity?*

'Sure,' he said. Luca made such a pathetic sight that Ralph couldn't begrudge him some old clothes. He turned to Luca, 'Come on then. The bathroom is up the stairs.' He turned and headed up, but looking over his shoulder he could see Luca had made no move to follow. The boy was just staring at him, open-mouthed and unblinking.

Ralph beckoned and pointed to the bathroom, mouthing 'shower' very slowly, but still nothing. Clearly this would be more difficult than they'd thought.

'Just lead him by the hand for goodness' sake Ralph,' said his dad, 'he doesn't understand English yet, so we'll just have to be patient with him.'

Ralph wasn't comfortable holding hands at the best of times, but this went double for strange putrid smelling Transylvanians. Unfortunately, he didn't have a pointy stick to hand that he could use to drive Luca up the stairs, so he didn't see any other options.

Ralph took Luca by his clammy hand and led him to the bathroom. Not trusting Luca to figure it out for himself, he turned on the light and got the shower running.

Luca just stood there. He didn't seem to have twigged that Ralph had put the shower on for him. Or perhaps he was just shy about getting undressed in front of Ralph. Ralph mimed taking off his clothes and pointed to the shower. Luca did not react. Ralph took hold of Luca's hand and held it under the hot water of the shower. 'You go in shower. Get warm,' he said, using the simplest language he could think of.

'Brrraiinns.'

Ralph was in shock for a moment. It was the first word he had heard Luca utter since he had arrived.

'What was that?' said Ralph, wondering whether he'd heard right.

'Brrraiinns,' said Luca again.

His voice was like a chainsaw caught on a metal wire, it ground against Ralph's ears. Despite Luca's strange voice and thick accent it was obvious what he was trying to say.

'It's not rain, it's a shower. It's similar though. We use it for washing,' he grabbed a bar of soap and imitated a washing motion.

No wonder he isn't getting in, thought Ralph. *He's been out in the freezing rain for goodness knows how long.*

It was for his own good though, so Ralph took matters into his own hands. Grabbing hold of Luca by the collar, he heaved him into the shower fully clothed.

Luca didn't resist, but he didn't try to wash himself either. Ralph grabbed the soap and an old scrubbing brush and began to scrub him from head to toe, working the soap into a lather and washing hard with the brush to get the stink off. When he was satisfied, he grabbed the shower head and hosed Luca down to rinse off any excess soap before pushing him out onto the bath mat, where he stood dripping.

While he was at it, Ralph decided he might as well go the whole hog and tackle Luca's monstrous gnashers. Ralph knew Americans mocked the standard of dental care in England. *If we're bad, the dental hygiene standards in Transylvania must be diabolical,* he thought.

Obviously, Luca didn't have a toothbrush of his own, but Ralph found an old one that he sometimes used to clean his football boots. He squirted out as much toothpaste as he could fit onto the bristles. He attacked Luca's mouth with gusto, scrubbing at Luca's teeth like the time he'd spilled paint on his dad's carpet and attempted to clean it up before he got back. As he worked the brush around the sharp pointed teeth, bits of rotting meat and gristle began to come away, giving off a foul stench. Ralph suspected it was the first-time fluoride had seen the inside of Luca's mouth. When he'd finished, Luca's teeth still didn't look any better, but it had done wonders for the stinky breath.

The next problem he had was Luca's dripping wet clothes. Ralph knew Imelda and dad would flip out if they realised he'd put Luca into the shower fully clothed, so he had to get him dry. He considered the airing cupboard but had to discount it for speed; it would take Luca all night to dry there. Towels would never work on wet clothes, so his only option was the hair dryer.

Ralph dragged Luca onto the landing, he found the hair dryer in Imelda's bedroom and began to blast Luca with it. He started at the feet and worked his way up. It was slow progress, but eventually he reached the top and aimed the dryer at Luca's hair. As he progressed methodically around, he realised he had been drying from underneath too much and had blown Luca's hair so it was standing vertical on the top of his head, making him seem taller and more forbidding than ever. Ralph hadn't got Luca completely dry, but he was okay for what Ralph had in mind. He scaled the ladder to his room, grabbed an old tracksuit from the pile of clothes he kept on the floor for easy access and scurried back down before Luca could wander off. He needn't have worried, Luca was standing in the exact spot Ralph had left him, the same vacant expression on his face. Ralph pulled Luca's arms into the tracksuit top and zipped it up. The trousers were going to be trickier but Ralph had picked a pair that had zips in the bottom so he wouldn't have to take Luca's shoes off. He dreaded to think what kind of state the Transylvanian's feet were in. He'd have inch long yellow claws for toenails if the rest of him was anything to go by. Ralph lifted Luca's foot and to his surprise Luca was being rather compliant, although of course he made no acknowledgement of what was going on or any effort to help dress himself. Ralph slipped the tracksuit bottoms over his feet and pulled them up.

Ralph stood back to appraise his handiwork. Luca still looked… odd. He had a face that wouldn't suit anything at all, and Victorian leather shoes would never work with a turquoise sports outfit. At least the smell had diminished, and Ralph felt that in certain areas he might be able to pass for an upstanding member of the community, although perhaps not in Great Merritt.

'You'll do,' he muttered, mostly to himself, feeling an unfamiliar sense of pride in the job he'd done with the makeover. Perhaps he had a future as a celebrity stylist. He was warming to Luca too. He liked the way the boy kept himself to himself. 'Come on then you,' he said to Luca, 'let's get you some food.'

Downstairs, Imelda had reheated the leftover dinner at which Ralph had turned up his nose. He felt guilty about that now after seeing how painfully thin Luca was. Imelda sat Luca at the table and placed a bowl of the Transylvanian offal soup in front of him. Again, Luca just sat there and Ralph wondered whether he'd be capable of feeding himself, but when Joshua made eating motions with his hands, Luca seemed to understand and looked down into his soup.

'Brrraiinns.'

'What did he say?' asked Joshua.

'I think he's saying rain. Sounds like brains, but I think it's his accent. He said it when I put the shower on for him earlier.'

'Oh, of course. That makes sense after he got soaked through. I wonder if he knows a bit of English after all, or if it's just that they have a similar word to us for rain. Fascinating stuff eh Ralph?' replied his dad. He rarely asked Ralph his opinion on whether something was fascinating, so Ralph assumed Dad was just trying to keep him on side while he sized up the new boy.

As they were chatting, Luca reached his hand into the soup bowl and found a particularly gristly looking piece of meat.

'Oh, sorry darling, that looks like a bad bit. Let me get you some more,' apologised Imelda.

'Brrraiinns,' said Luca, shoving the meat into his mouth and tearing at it like a feasting hyena.

Imelda's face lit up. 'Oh, he likes it!' she gushed. 'I told you he wouldn't be as fussy as you British children.'

Ralph watched Luca chew at the meat in his hands and wondered about the other ways in which the boy might differ from British children.

'Ralph, you might as well go back to bed,' said his dad. 'Luca can sleep on the sofa tonight and we'll set him up in your room tomorrow.'

'OK,' said Ralph, wondering if he'd be able to sleep after all the excitement. Watching Luca eating his stew was going to be enough to give him nightmares if he did.

4
A Hard Lesson

Ralph shoved the toast into his mouth, greedily forcing the whole slice in. He wanted to make sure he had a good breakfast before Luca started eating again and put him off his food.

Imelda appeared in the kitchen looking as pleased as punch, closely followed by a shambling Luca. Luca was wearing Ralph's school uniform from the year before. It was several sizes too small for him, even on his bone-thin frame, and added to his bizarre look.

'Doesn't he look a darling?' said Imelda. She gave Luca's hair an affectionate ruffle.

'Very smart,' agreed Joshua. 'I think we may have a future head boy on our hands here, Imelda. We'd better head off though, we're running late,' he said, putting his coat.

Imelda bundled Luca up in a bear hug.

'My little boy on his first day at school,' she shot a look at Ralph. 'You look after him, Ralphie. I know what those school bullies are like, always picking on anyone different.'

Ralph had already considered this and was planning to stay as far away from Luca as possible. He didn't want anyone to associate him with Luca's weirdness.

'I'll do my best,' he said.

'OK let's go,' said Joshua. 'To the Cribbmobile!' His attempt at a joke did not raise so much as a smile between the three of them but Joshua remained unperturbed. 'Lead the way, Ralph,' he said.

Imelda wiped away a tear of pride as she watched Joshua and the boys head to the car. They were a proper family at last.

* * *

The school that Ralph attended and at which Mr Cribbens taught was called Riverside Academy. It was a shabby old three-storey building with ancient windows that the wind whistled through in the winter, meaning the school had a permanent draught and a lingering smell of damp. A high green fence with spikes across the top surrounded the grounds and made Ralph feel like he was in a high-security prison as he stared out of the window, daydreaming during lessons.

As they pulled into the school car park, Ralph stayed low in his seat, keeping a careful eye out for any stragglers who hadn't made it to Registration on time. As soon as they stopped, he leapt from the car and sprinted for the school doors. It was bad enough arriving with Dad, and he certainly didn't want to answer questions about Luca from other kids.

'He's very keen,' Joshua remarked to Luca as they watched the door crash shut behind Ralph. 'Your brother is very conscientious about his schoolwork. A stickler for punctuality. Shall we get going to the Reception Office? Every minute we waste you could be learning something!'

Luca replied with a grunt that appeared to indicate his agreement.

As they approached the reception desk Mr Cribbens failed to notice the brief flicker of alarm on the face of Miss Welton, the Receptionist.

'Hello there Miss Welton,' Joshua beamed at the receptionist. 'I'm here to register my son. For school.'

'For school?' The Receptionist took a moment to regain her composure. 'Then I suppose you've come to the right place. I didn't know you had another son, Mr Cribbens?'

'Yes,' Joshua thrust Luca forward, every inch the proud father. 'This is Luca. He's come to us from Transylvania.'

'Hello Luca,' she said, trying not to show her revulsion. The boy was salivating over something. 'And will Luca be staying with you on a permanent basis? Are you his guardian, Mr Cribbens?'

'I'm his Father. We've adopted him. Saved him from a life of poverty.'

'And you have all the relevant paperwork with you?' she peered at them suspiciously.

'Paperwork? Errm, yes, well, he only arrived yesterday so I'm afraid the paperwork is… processing… yes processing.'

'Riiiiight,' she said, still staring at them with a quizzical look on her face. 'Well, I'm sure you know we can't let him start school without the correct documentation.'

'Well, of course,' Joshua stalled for time while he concocted his response. 'Obviously, with me being a teacher, there couldn't possibly be anything untoward going on. And, here's a thought, what if Ralph acted as a chaperon? You know, he could stick with Luca the whole time, make sure he doesn't cause any bother. Whaddayareckon?'

Miss Welton weighed up the options. On the one hand, Mr Cribbens was an annoying buffoon, and she didn't feel like doing him any favours. On the other, they didn't pay her enough to deal with hassle like this.

'Very well. Luca can join Ralph's class. I'm sure it will be helpful for him to get a handle on the ways of the school and understand how things work. Unfortunately, we can't provide an English tutor for him, so you'll have to teach him at home,' she glanced at Luca's expressionless face. 'I'm sure he'll pick it up in no time,' she fibbed. 'Children always do!'

While Joshua Cribbens headed off to prepare for his own lessons, Miss Welton took charge of Luca.

'Come with me, Luca. Let's see if we can get you to your class before they finish registration,' she said, giving him the sweetest smile she could muster up.

Miss Welton placed her hand gingerly on his back to hurry him. She didn't want to touch him, but this boy was clearly a shambling dilly dallier. She knew the sort well, and he'd never make it to class without a little encouragement.

* * *

Ralph took his place in Reg, slipping in next to Sunny, relieved that he'd made it in without being spotted with Luca.

The general pre-reg chit chat was dying down as their form teacher, Mr Hulkington, started the daily routine of calling out the register. Mr Hulkington was known to the children as "The Hulk". The Hulk was a short and, on first glance, unassuming man, but he had a booming voice that could fill a room and it was never a good idea to make him angry.

41

'AHMED?'

'Sir.'

'BROWN?'

'Sir.'

'BRISTOW?'

'Yes Sir.'

'CAAN?'

'Sir.'

'Can't more like!' bellowed The Hulk, as he did every day.

The class fell about laughing as one, as they did every day.

Unlike every other day, the classroom door opened at that point and Miss Welton crept in. Followed closely, to Ralph's horror and to everyone else's curiosity, by Luca, who was looking even more dishevelled than when they had left home an hour ago.

Miss Welton whispered to The Hulk, explaining everything about Luca that she'd learned from Mr Cribbens. The Hulk raised his eyebrows and whispered something back before nodding, all the while looking daggers at Ralph.

Ralph swallowed, and tried to look as if he was as surprised to see this new boy as everybody else. Miss Welton turned and left, closing the door quietly behind her, leaving Luca standing at the front looking bewildered.

The Hulk let Luca stand there like an exhibit at the Chamber of Horrors while he finished taking the register. He didn't like his routine being interrupted, even by other staff members.

'Well then,' he finally said.

'I expect you are wondering what this,' he gestured at Luca, 'is all about.'

'It turns out we are lucky to be welcoming a new member of the class this morning. Ladies and Gentlemen, allow me to do you the honour of introducing you to Luca! Say hello boys and girls,' he growled.

'Hello Luca,' mumbled the class.

Luca just stood there, looking like he hadn't noticed the rest of the class.

'Oh yes, I forgot to mention, he doesn't speak a word of English.'

Ralph wondered if he might get away with it after all. If Luca couldn't communicate with the other kids and he made a point of not making eye contact or even being within 10 yards of him, how could any of them know Luca was his "brother"?

'I said, he doesn't speak English, does he… Ralph?' Ralph's hope of escape died as thirty-two heads turned to focus on him.

The Hulk seemed to take Ralph's noncommittal shrug as a green light to give the class the full story.

'Luca here, has been imported into the country by the Cribbens family who, by all accounts, whisked him from a life of toil and turmoil in darkest Transylvania. They'll be adopting him, although I understand the paperwork is still "pending" at the moment, so for all intents and purposes Luca is Ralph's brother.'

Ralph was not oblivious to the heavy sarcasm in The Hulk's voice, but he was more concerned with the sniggering that was sweeping across the room.

The bell went for the end of registration and the class moved for the doors; whispers and stolen glances at Ralph and Luca replaced the usual conversations that picked up after The Hulk finished taking the register.

The Hulk grabbed Ralph's arm as he tried to skulk out of the door.

'I want you to buddy up with your brother. Make sure nothing happens to him and he ends up in all the right places. Remember, he is your responsibility so don't let him out of your sight.'

'Sir,' nodded Ralph. 'C'mon then,' he said to Luca, gesturing him towards the door.

* * *

By what Ralph could only assume was a miracle, most of the day passed without incident. Ralph and Sunny hid Luca away in the library for morning break and for most of lunch, and he caused no major problems. There were a few glances in their direction as Luca tore into the ham from his sandwiches like a hyena, tossing the bread aside as if it were packaging, but overall Ralph thought the morning had gone as well as it could have done.

After lunch, though, was Design and Technology. That was the one Ralph had been dreading the most. That was the subject his dad taught.

'Come on in, come on in! Don't dawdle!' said Mr Cribbens as he ushered the year sevens into his classroom.

'Take your seats, Plomp, put that away you disgusting creature,' he snapped at Richard Plomp who was clearing out his nose with a finger of Kit-Kat. 'You should have finished your lunch in the dining hall.'

44

Ralph tugged Luca by his sleeve when he made no move to enter the classroom.

'Come on, boys! Luca, I'm expecting you to be good at this. No doubt you're a chip off the old block. Not sure what happened to Ralph though!'

Ralph dragged Luca to the nearest available seat as quickly as he could to avoid any further attention. He was already hearing mocking sniggers coming from the back of the room. Plomp and his pals Breezeblock and Parsnip were certain to have something to say the next time they caught him outside the classroom. They weren't the type to pass up the opportunity of giving someone a hard time.

'This week,' said Mr Cribbens as he walked to the front of the class and began his lesson. 'Is particularly exciting as we'll be learning about the saw.'

He smiled and held his saw aloft. 'A mainstay of any toolkit, the humble saw, has been used by humans since at least the time of the ancient Egyptians. With a saw and a bit of elbow grease we can start the process of turning a hunk of old wood into a chair, a table or even a cricket bat. Who would like to help me demonstrate?'

Sunny's hand shot into the air.

'Up you come then, Miss Brightwell.'

'Now then,' said Mr Cribbens as Sunny picked up the saw that looked so old the ancient Egyptians could have used it themselves. She positioned herself next to the piece of wood that Mr Cribbens had set up in a vice at the end of a bench. 'We simply run the saw back and forth across the top of wood and you'll see that the teeth bite on each motion causing—'

GRRRRRRRRRR!!!

45

Sunny had discarded the old wooden hand saw and whipped a whirring blade from beneath her jacket. Ralph covered his mouth, realising that Sunny must have seen this as an opportunity to show off one of her own inventions. She hefted the screeching machine over the wood before setting it down on top. It didn't so much as cut through the wood as obliterate it, spraying splinters around the classroom.

'Stop!' shouted Mr Cribbens as Sunny's homemade saw started tearing through the workbench itself.

'I can't!' squealed Sunny, her voice vibrating from the power of the saw. 'If I let-t-t g-o-o of the ha-n-n-dle I'll lo-o-se con-trol of my Wonder Saw! The but-t-ton is on-n-n the to-p-p!'

Mr Cribbens grabbed Sunny's wrists, needing all his might to keep the Wonder Saw from propelling itself and Sunny wildly around the classroom.

'Ralph, Lu-c-ca, help us out here would-d-d you?' he said, his voice vibrating like he was holding a jackhammer.

'But, I…' The lethal looking Wonder Saw seemed like it would shake loose from their grasp any second. He looked across at Luca, who stared impassively at the scene in front of them. A droplet of saliva quivered on the edge of Luca's lip. Ralph realised he would not get any help there and gritted his teeth, ready to leap into action. And he would have done. But before he could drag himself from his seat, Bernard Laboon was already flying past his desk. With a graceful dive Bernard sailed past Ralph, his outstretched fingers brushing the button on Sunny's lethal invention and disabling it before it could do any more damage.

'Thank you, Bernard,' said Mr Cribbens, letting out a sigh of relief. 'At least we have someone in this class we can rely on in a tricky situation.' He shot a glance at Ralph.

'No worries, sir,' said Bernard, flashing a smile. The other kids sometimes called him Bernard "Kaboom". When he played football, he had a shot that was so powerful it was like he had fired it from a cannon. He was also the laziest kid in the class. He always looked like he'd just rolled out of bed, whatever time it was. The rumour was he could sleep with his eyes open, so he could doze through lessons without getting caught. All the commotion must have interfered with his beauty sleep and he'd decided to intervene, so he could get some peace for his afternoon nap.

'My hero!' said Sunny. She took her seat next to Ralph, giving him an icy glance as she did so.

'Well! I think I'll keep hold of this… device for now, Miss Brightwell. I think we've had quite enough of a demonstration for one day!' said Mr Cribbens, who had regained his composure. 'Very innovative, I must say, though perhaps the design needs a little refinement.' Mr Cribbens was a big fan of Sunny's inventions. She was the only student who ever did any design and technology work in her own time, so he didn't like to discourage her, even after she had turned half his classroom into firewood.

Not one to be dismayed by such a minor mishap, Mr Cribbens continued the lesson as planned. Ralph always paired with Sunny for group work, but this time she had made a beeline for Bernard as soon as the practical part of the lesson had started, leaving Ralph stuck with Luca for his partner. The task was to produce a bird box from a sheet of plywood by cutting it with a saw and nailing it back together using the hammer technique Mr Cribbens had shown them the previous week.

'Do you want to saw or hammer?' Ralph asked Luca.

'Brrraiinns,' muttered Luca.

'That's fine, I'll saw then,' agreed Ralph, pretending Luca had said something that made sense for once.

Ralph pencilled the shape of the bird box onto the plywood and then, using his weight to hold it steady on the edge of the workbench, he sawed the pieces out, taking care to make sure he followed the lines he'd drawn.

'Your turn then,' he said to Luca, handing him the hammer and a tin full of nails.

Luca just continued to stare into space, making no move to take the tools from Ralph. *What is wrong with this freak?* Ralph thought. *I know he doesn't speak the language that well, but surely, it's obvious what you do with a hammer and nails? And this was the kid who they wanted to help Dad landscape the garden!*

'I tell you what…' Ralph took hold of Luca by the shoulders and moved him around so he was standing facing the workbench. 'You hold the nails steady and I'll tap them into the wood.' He took Luca's hand and pressed it down on an intersection where two pieces would connect to make the bird house. He placed a nail between Luca's finger and thumb and pressed them together. By what must have been sheer chance, the strange boy held it just where Ralph needed it.

Ralph glanced up and spotted Sunny smiling as she worked with Bernard. Or rather, Sunny was doing the work while Bernard leaned back in his chair with his hands behind his head. *At least I actually help when she works with me,* he thought. *Why work with that lazy slob? It's not my fault he got to the button before me.*

He brought the hammer down onto the nail and raised it for another strike. As he started swinging, though, he realised that the wood had moved off centre. He sighed. 'Luca, you need to hold it in the same… hmm.' He looked down at the wood. *Strange*. Luca wasn't gripping it but where he moved his hand, the wood followed. At first, Ralph thought Luca had done some sort of magic trick, but as he focused on what was happening, he realised with growing horror that he'd somehow nailed Luca's hand to the birdhouse.

He wasn't the only one to realise it either. Ralph glanced up to see the entire class staring in his direction.

'I think you've got something stuck to your hand Luca,' Breezeblock said from the back of the class with a dry chuckle.

There was a brief pause before two of the girls started screaming, and one boy fainted.

Mr Cribbens rubbed at his temple. Suddenly, he'd come down with a splitting headache. 'Class dismissed,' he said, sounding thoroughly annoyed. 'Ralph, Luca, stay with me. We'll be making a brief detour to the hospital on the way home.'

5
Hide and Shriek

'Honestly Imelda, you've never seen anything like it!' said Joshua Cribbens as he scooped up another spoonful of cornflakes.

'Joshua, you are a joker!' chuckled Imelda.

'He's not joking,' said Ralph as he covered a yawn. They'd been at the hospital until late into the night, so Ralph was thanking his lucky stars it was the weekend. If he'd had school today, he'd have been about as energetic as Luca. 'The doctor pulled the nail out of his hand without a drop of blood. Said it must have somehow missed all the veins and arteries. One in a billion chance, apparently.'

'It sounds impossible! I guess he is just a very lucky boy,' she said, reaching down and giving Luca's lank hair a ruffle before she pulled a face that looked like she regretted it, and wiped her hand on her apron. Luca meanwhile was munching his way through his second plate of sausages.

'Hmm, well, I'm not sure how lucky you can be when your own brother is hammering nails into your hand,' said Joshua, glaring across the table at Ralph. 'Ralph just seems incapable of using any kind of tool. If you gave that boy a tape measure, he'd take his own eye out with it! Absolutely useless.'

Ralph squirmed in his seat listening to his father's criticism.

'Well, all's well that ends well, I suppose. No harm done,' said Imelda. 'We have a fun day planned today so let's just make sure we enjoy ourselves.'

* * *

Much to Ralph's relief, by the time they pulled up at the country park for the PTA Autumn half term picnic (that the committee insisted on holding in October despite the rain they got every other year) Mr Cribbens seemed to have cheered up.

'What a lovely day!' said Joshua Cribbens, getting out of the car with a spring in his step. 'Nothing like a lungful of fresh country air to get the blood pumping, eh? And the sun is shining for a change. Perfect weather for a barbeque!'

Mr Cribbens loved a barbeque. He fancied himself as a master burger flipper, and his special ribs were renowned throughout the area (or so he believed). He had a set of barbecue tongs which he'd had imported from Japan and reckoned they gave him an edge over the other dads when it came to producing a truly succulent sausage.

Ralph spotted Sunny playing some kind of chasing game with the other kids on the edge of a wooded area and made his way over towards them across the field.

'You just wait a moment,' said Ralph's dad. 'Aren't you forgetting something?'

Ralph rolled his eyes and let out a soft sigh. 'Come on then Luca.'

'Be back here in an hour for the barbeque,' said Mr Cribbens. 'And stay out of trouble for once!'

'Oh, they'll be back soon enough,' said Imelda with a smile. 'My little Luca has such an appetite he won't miss his lunch for anything!'

Ralph stomped across the field to where Sunny and the other kids were hanging out. They were playing a game where one team were runners and the other team were chasers. Once the chasers caught everyone on the running team, the game was over. Sunny looked like she'd already been caught, so was sitting the rest of the game out waiting for a new round to start.

'Ralphie!' she called. Ralph had been worried she'd still be annoyed with him for not jumping in to save her during yesterday's incident with the Wonder Saw but Sunny wasn't the type to hold a grudge. 'I wasn't sure if you'd make it after yesterday. Luca is your hand ok?' she said, turning to the pale quiet boy.

'Brrraiinns,' said Luca.

'He keeps saying that,' said Ralph. 'I guess it must be Transylvanian for hello or something.'

'Ah, of course. *Brayynz* to you too, Luca,' said Sunny with her biggest smile. 'You know Ralph, we really should try to teach him some English. The poor boy has no idea what's going on most of the time.'

'What have you got in mind?'

'We just need to show him what different words mean. Look here.'

Sunny turned to a nearby bush and plucked a leaf from it. She twizzled it in her fingers and began waving it in Luca's face.

'This is pointless,' said Ralph. 'He's clearly brain dead.'

Sunny ignored him and carried on with her lesson.

'Luca,' she said pointedly, taking to her new role as schoolmistress like a duck to water. 'This is a leaf. Leaf. Can you say leaf? L-e-a-f.'

For a moment it appeared Luca might respond. He opened his mouth as if to speak but with a sudden motion he darted his head forward, snapping his jaws shut around the leaf. Another two millimeters and he would have taken Sunny's fingers with it.

'He must have thought it was food,' said Sunny. 'Silly Luca, we're not having the barbecue until later you know!'

'I don't know Sunny,' said Ralph, shaking his head. 'There's something not right about him if you ask me.'

'Ralphie, don't be nasty. He's come to a new country and everything is strange to him. It's going to take time to settle in.'

'New game!' a voice called from the woods.

'Come on, let's join in,' said Sunny. 'Luca, you can be a chaser with me. Ralph, you'd better join the runners.'

'Ready, set… GO!' called Billy Chewswell. Billy was always organising games like this.

'See you later,' said Ralph, as he dashed off into the woods.

Ralph took off at a sprint. He charged through the trees until he was well out of sight. Branches whipped at his face and he battled through bushes. He kept going until he was out of puff. Ralph stopped in a clearing and sucked a couple of deep breaths into his lungs. Ralph wasn't the sporty type, so he didn't get much exercise. He wiped sweat from his brow and realised a branch must have cut him as he had blood on his fingers. He looked back, expecting to be well away from the group, but he could still see the green grass of the picnic area through the trees. *Not a bad thing*, he thought. If he got too deep into the woods, people would forget he was part of the game, so what would be the point? Even here, just a few hundred yards from the picnic, the woods were so quiet it was eerie. He couldn't hear the bustle of the parents chatting in the barbeque area. The trees absorbed sound, so it got quiet fast.

Ralph leaned against a tree, trying to get his breath back. He wasn't sure why he'd taken off so fast, but it felt good to get the blood pumping around his body and feel the rush of exhilaration as he dashed through the trees.

Off to his left, Ralph saw a flash of colour. A second later another followed it. The chasers must have spotted a kid from his team, he realised. Ralph hunkered down to make sure he wasn't spotted and watched to see what happened.

As the kids got closer, Ralph could hear their screams of joy as they rushed through the trees. The first one moved fast, darting between the trunks and ducking under the low branches. The pursuer had a different motion. They pressed forward, moving at a slower pace but relentless. Rather than dodge the obstacles, they went through them, shambling forward, never stopping.

Luca! Ralph realised. *At least he's got into the game*, thought Ralph. But as he watched, he realised something wasn't quite right. The other kid seemed frantic. It looked like it was Billy Chewswell, the kid who had organised the game. Billy was trying to scrabble up a slope, but with the loose leaves and stones he kept slipping back, his knees bled where he must have fallen over. He was still screaming but there was a note of panic in the sound now as Billy turned to face Luca who loomed over him, his fingers reaching for Billy like claws, his mouth open wide exposing his pointed yellow teeth.

'Luca! What are young doing?!' shouted Ralph 'You can't…'

Luca looked around, his cold black eyes turning on Ralph. Saliva was drooling from his mouth in a long trail that dripped past his chin.

'He's mental!' quivered Billy, getting to his feet. 'He tried to bite me!' Billy staggered away from Luca before turning and sprinting off as fast as he could, leaving Ralph alone in the woods with his brother.

'Luca, you can't go around doing that. We're supposed to be playing to be a game!' said Ralph, pointing an angry finger after the fleeing Billy.

But Luca was lurching towards Ralph now, his eyes deep and dark as cavern pools. His bony hands reaching for Ralph's neck.

'Brrraiinns,' Luca muttered, taking another lurching step forward.

Ralph tried to back away, but his foot caught in the loop of a tree root and he tumbled backwards, cracking his head hard on the dirt floor.

As the world spun, Ralph could just make out Luca's pale lips moving close to his throat. *This is it*, Ralph thought. *He's going to eat me.*

A flash of red exploded before Ralph's eyes, and Luca stumbled to the side. He lay there groaning in a heap while Ralph staggered to his feet, wondering what had happened.

A bright red boxing glove lay on the floor with what looked like sand spilling from the wrist opening. Ralph stared at it in thankful confusion.

'Don't I get a thank you?' Sunny stepped out of the trees behind Ralph.

'Sunny! I've never been so happy to see you!' said Ralph.

'Yes you have Ralphie, you're always *delighted* to see me,' Sunny replied curtly, but she had a wisp of a smile on her face.

Sunny reached down to retrieve the boxing glove. 'The Punchatron 2000,' she said in a matter-of-fact tone. 'It's still a work in progress, but seems to be shaping up. That's the first time it's hit the target to be honest, but it's a start.' Sunny opened the baggy sleeve of her jacket to show Ralph what was inside. 'Compressed air canister. Only good for one punch, but the reach is knockout.'

'It's definitely one of your better inventions,' said Ralph. He turned and nodded towards where Luca was getting to his feet. 'What are we going to do about him?'

Sunny flicked her curly blonde hair away from her face. 'I'm not sure, but I think he needs help. The poor boy must have had a very difficult past.'

'You're not kidding,' said Ralph. 'Very difficult, very difficult indeed. In fact, I'm pretty sure he's, err, dead.'

'Ralph, don't be horrible! Your poor brother! I know he's very difficult but he—'

'Sunny look,' Ralph took a comic from his pocket and pointed at a picture. In the scene, a man was battling a horde of slobbering creatures. Their bodies were rotting and twisted. Some were missing limbs or bits of skin.

But they were all staggering towards the man with an obvious intention of devouring his brains.

'Sunny,' Ralph repeated, pointing again, his voice almost a whisper. 'I think Luca might be… he might be a zombie!'

* * *

By the time they'd wandered back to the picnic, using a stick to keep Luca a safe distance away, the pale boy's earlier bloodlust seemed to have receded.

'It must have been the running and chasing,' said Sunny. 'It got him all worked up.'

Ralph nodded. 'Me and Billy both had cuts on us too. Not to mention he can probably smell the meat from the barbecue.'

As if to confirm Ralph's suggestion, Luca launched himself at a half-eaten burger as they passed a picnic table. Ahead, Ralph could see his parents engaged in a furious argument with a larger group of parents.

'I'm sure this is all a big misunderstanding!' said Imelda, shaking her head. 'He would never—'

'He tried to bite my son!' shouted Billy Chewswell's dad.

Billy was cowering behind his dad's legs, still trembling from his ordeal. When he spotted Luca approaching with Ralph and Sunny, he screamed and scrambled back. 'Keep him away from me!' he cried, backing away. 'He knows, he saw it all!' Billy continued, pointing at Ralph.

Joshua Cribbens turned to his son, 'Ralph, tell this ignoramus what happened! It was an accident, of course.'

Ralph assessed the situation. He could have voiced his theory about Luca being a zombie, but looking at the angry faces of his parents and the other mums and dads, it probably wasn't the best time to raise the topic.

'I think Luca got a bit carried away. I think it's the language barrier,' he looked at Billy. 'Billy, Luca's really sorry. The games they play in Transylvania are rougher than over here. He thought the aim of the game was to knock you over.'

'But he was trying to bite me!' insisted Billy.

'He was pretending to be a wolf. That's what they play over there. Err, werewolves and victims, I think it's called.' replied Ralph, thinking on his feet.

'Well, there you go,' said Joshua Cribbens. 'You heard it from the horse's mouth. Come on boys, we're leaving. We won't stay here for you to insult our family.' He scooped a plateful of chicken legs off the grill and stomped back to the car with Imelda scurrying after him.

'Come on then Luca,' Ralph impaled a sausage with the stick he'd used to herd Luca toward the picnic and wafted it in front of Luca's face.

'Brrraiinns,' uttered the zombie, reaching out to grab the sausage and staggering after Ralph.

Sunny took Ralph by his arm before he got any further and leaned in to whisper in his ear. 'Ralphie, don't you think you should tell your parents about… you know,' she nodded in Luca's direction.

'I suppose I'm going to have to. But the question is, how do I do that without them blowing their tops? Luca can do no wrong in their eyes.'

Sunny looked at Joshua Cribbens as he got into the car and slammed his door shut behind him. 'Hmm, maybe you could write them an anonymous letter?'

Ralph considered that for a moment, wondering if it might work. 'They'd recognise my writing,' he said sadly, just as Mr Cribbens started leaning on the car horn. It was his own gentle way of speeding the boys back to the car.

6
Pet Detectives

Over the next few weeks, Ralph got used to the idea of having Luca around, and the idea that Luca was some kind of zombie faded from his thoughts.

Luca had moved into the attic room with Ralph. his dad had knocked together a makeshift bunk bed out of old bits of timber and Ralph had ended up with the top bunk. It was impossible to climb to Ralph's bunk without the whole contraption swaying from side to side, so he felt fairly safe in the unlikely event that Luca was an undead creature after all. His bunk was also very close to the ceiling and was only accessible via one end. The two long sides almost touched the ceiling, but the bed sat in the centre of the attic, so the slope of the roof allowed him to sit up. The head end of the bed rested against the wall, blocking entry from that side. That meant the only way onto the top bunk was to clamber up using the stepladder at the foot end, and wriggle like a worm through the opening. When Ralph wanted to change his bedsheets, he needed to pull the entire mattress down and change them on the floor before lifting the fully made mattress up and sliding it back through the gap in the frame. The good news for Ralph was that the times when he felt the need to change his sheets were exceedingly rare. In fact, that need was yet to arise since he'd moved to the top bunk.

Luca himself required very little sleep. He was rarely in his bunk, instead preferring to spend most of the night standing facing the wall, muttering to himself in his strange guttural language. Ralph had looked up the strange 'brrraiinns' word he kept saying in a Transylvanian dictionary but hadn't been able to find it. He wondered whether it wasn't Transylvanian at all. It was likely Luca knew a little English, so Ralph wondered if he was complaining about how it rained all the time. He was always saying it, whatever the weather, but Ralph wasn't sure what else it could mean.

Luca had shown none of the aggression he'd displayed at the picnic since that day, in fact he'd been quiet and contained. He never approached Ralph and tried to start a conversation or ask a question or play. Ralph had tried chatting to him a few times, but Luca's response was never more than a doleful 'brrraiinns'.

He'd never directly asked his parents about whether it was possible that Luca could be a zombie, but he's tried to raise the subject in a round-about way a few times.

'Dad?' he asked his father one Saturday morning while Joshua Cribbens was getting ready for his Saturday morning rollerblading lesson. (Mr Cribbens never missed a rollerblade session come rain or shine, although he had once converted his blades to ice skates during a cold snap by screwing a pair of carving knives to the wheels).

'Make it quick, Ralph. You can see I'm heading out for a roll,' said, Mr Cribbens strapping on an elbow pad.

'Well, I was just wondering about Luca. I mean, I know he's new and all but… Do you think there is anything… well, anything… err… strange about him?'

'Strange? I don't know what you mean.'

'Well, he never speaks unless he's saying "brrraiinns". He only ever eats meat, the more undercooked the better.

I caught him trying to eat a pack of frozen sausages straight out of the freezer the other day. And all he ever does is shuffle about with a blank expression on his face. And let's not forget what happened at the picnic… '

'Ralph, I've told you we will forget what happened at the picnic,' Mr Cribbens put a comforting arm around his son, which had the immediate effect of making Ralph feel uncomfortable. 'Listen, I know that Luca coming here has been difficult for you. You're used to being the number one son. *Numero uno!* And now you have to fight to get noticed. After all, your brother has a big personality, so it's easy to get overlooked. What you must remember Ralph is that it's hard for him too. He's come here from another country. He doesn't speak the language; the culture is alien to him. You just need to give him a chance. Ok buddy?'

'Since when do you call me buddy?'

'The point is, you need to ease off on your brother. Yes, I know he seems a little slow sometimes, but it's a difficult situation to come into. Now Imelda and I understand the language is an issue, so we're getting some proper English lessons for him. There is a student at the university from Transylvania; I've asked her to come over and tutor him a couple of nights each week. I'm sure once that happens we'll see some real progress. I tell you what. How about we get takeaway from that new gumbo-to-go place on the weekend?'

'Gumbo?! What on earth is gumbo?'

'Well… I'm not exactly sure. I think it's some kind of spicy soup they eat in America and the Caribbean. Word on the street is it's spectacular, and Imelda is desperate to try it, but it's not my sort of thing. As you know, I'm more of a cheese on toast man. Now if that's all, I must be off or I'll be late for my roll.' With that Joshua Cribbens got to his feet and glided majestically through the door and down the street, leaving Ralph as confused as he'd been when the conversation started.

On the second morning of the half term break, Ralph lay in his bed enjoying not having to worry about school or his brother for a couple of days. He was idly flicking through a comic, just like he'd spent the entire previous day doing when the doorbell rang.

'Ralph!' Imelda's voice shrieked up the stairs. He was two floors up, but she had a voice like a smoke alarm. 'Your little girlfriend is here for you.'

'She's not my girlfriend,' he muttered as he slid through the small opening to let himself out of his bunk bed and made his way downstairs.

'Morning Ralphie. You're not still in bed, are you?' Sunny stood on the doorstep wearing pink leggings, a bright green cardigan and her favourite scarf which had pictures of little giraffes on it. She was looking way too perky for this time in the morning and she'd tied her wild yellow hair back in a ponytail which was most unlike her. It meant she already had plans.

'I'm not now,' Ralph replied with a yawn.

'Look at this Ralphie,' she thrust a bundle of papers into his hand.

'What's this?' Ralph said. It looked like a pile of missing pet posters she'd ripped down from lampposts on the way over.

'It's a pile of missing pet posters. I ripped them down from lampposts on the way over,' she said, looking at him like he should be excited about this for some reason.

63

'Ralph look. They're all different pets. Don't you see? There's a petnapper on the loose!'

Ralph flicked through the posters. There were all sorts, some handwritten by tearful loving owners, some typed, some laminated. Posters for cats, posters for dogs, posters for rabbits, tortoises, chinchillas and chickens. There was even one for a seven-legged tarantula whose owner swore it couldn't have got far, as it could only walk around in circles.

'OK.' said Ralph. 'But what's this got to do with us?'

'It's a project you dummy. Something to keep us occupied for half-term. And look…' Sunny started flicking through the posters, pointing to the rewards that a lot of them offered. 'If we can solve this, we'll get all these rewards. Imagine how many tools I could buy with that. Think of all the comics you could buy? I mean, I'd do it just to find the poor missing pets, but I know you aren't as generous of spirit as I am Ralphie.'

'Hey, I'm generous, I—'

'So you're in?' said Sunny.

'Er well yes, I'm in, I suppose.' said Ralph. He felt tricked, but it *did* sound like it could be an adventure.

'If you two are going out, can you keep an eye out for Luca?' Imelda called from the living room. She had her feet up with her favourite show about the *Housewives of the Home Counties* on the television and was tucking into a large block of chocolate. 'He's wandered off again and you know how I worry about him.'

'OK,' said Ralph through gritted teeth. Luca had taken to disappearing lately, and it was always Ralph who got tasked with bringing him home. He rarely went far; it was like he'd accidentally shambled out of the door when someone left it open, but it was becoming an annoyance.

Ralph ran upstairs, whizzed his toothbrush around his mouth, put on some fresh-ish clothes and headed back down to find Sunny sitting on his doorstep chewing gum. 'Are you ready yet?' she said before blowing a melon-sized bubble.

Ralph popped it with his finger, bursting the sticky gum all over Sunny's face. 'More ready than you,' he said with a grin.

Sunny was unconcerned as she peeled the gum off her face and popped it in in her mouth. 'Then let's roll, Detective Cribbens! We have a crime to solve *and* some very cute animals to rescue!'

* * *

'Where do you think we should start?' said Ralph. They'd meandered up Bushy Lane away from Ralph's house towards the edge of town and were resting on a fallen tree. Behind them, houses became sparser until they melted into nothing but fields in the distance.

Sunny chewed her lip as she flicked through the posters. 'Ahh, look at this one. So cute!' she held up a picture of a puppy whose tongue was lolling so far out its mouth it looked like it would trip itself over.

'It looks like it's swallowed a scarf. I was asking about the plan. I'm assuming you have one, seeing how you started this wild goose chase?'

'Ralph, the missing geese are not wild, they belonged to Mrs Jessop. And yes, I have a plan,' she whipped a marker pen and a rectangle of paper from her back pocket and unfolded a map of the Great Merritt area. 'If we mark each of the addresses of the missing pets on

65

this map, it should allow us to triangulate the area within which the criminal operates,' Sunny began flicking through the posters at a frantic pace, scribbling x's on the maps whenever she saw an address or location. Eventually she added a cross for the final poster, placed the map on a tree stump and stood back to take in the pattern. 'Hmm..' she said, sounding disappointed. 'I'm not sure this tells us much. Other than there are lots of missing pets in Great Merritt, as we already knew.'

Ralph was looking over her shoulder. 'Wait a second. Give me the pen,' he began drawing lines criss-crossing the paper, working out the midpoint of where all the disappearances took place. He was no mathematician, but he had an instinct for geometry and maps. He stood back and circled an area in the map's corner. 'We should start looking somewhere in this area. That's the centre, so it's likely the petnapper operates out of somewhere near here.'

'That's convenient,' replied Sunny. 'That's exactly where we are now.'

'So, we're at the very centre of pet vanishings,' said Ralph, with a puzzled air. 'Right here on Bushy Lane. That's crazy, I mean, I know a couple of people have lost pets around here. Mrs Bagshot lost her rabbit the other day. She called him Sir Henry Hoppington. She told Imelda it was as if he'd just vanished from his cage. Sir Henry used to be a magician's rabbit, so she'd just assumed he was up to his old tricks again. Mrs Bagshot was devastated when he never came back though.'

'Yeah, but Bushy Lane is just the start of it,' said Sunny, studying the map. 'Everything radiates out from here.'

Ralph looked thoughtful for a moment. 'You don't think… Luca couldn't have something to do with this, could he?' Ralph nibbled on his fingernails. He did this when he was worried, but never chewed them off completely.

'I thought you'd gone off your zombie idea? You said he'd calmed down since what happened on the picnic?'

'Well, he has calmed down. But… what if the reason he's calmed down is he's found a way to calm *himself* down?'

'What on earth are you talking about, Ralphie? You're making my head spin,' said Sunny, looking bemused.

'I mean, what if he's discovered a way to satisfy his appetite? It sounds crazy but could he have been *eating the pets*?'

Sunny's green eyes widened with horror. 'He can't have!'

Ralph looked her in the eyes and gave a slow nod of his head. 'It makes sense, Sunny. Think about it, he hasn't needed to take a chunk out of any people since the picnic because he's been gobbling up the local pets.'

Sunny covered her mouth with her hand. 'Oh my goodness, Ralphie. That's awful. And what happens when he—'

Ralph finished her sentence for her. 'What happens when he can't get enough pets? Judging by the number of disappearances we might be about to find out.'

A rustling in the trees made them turn, and a strange man stumbled into the clearing. He was wearing a ragged red t-shirt with the word '*Thriller*' written on it and ripped jeans and looked like he had spent the evening sleeping under a bush.

'Are you ok?' Sunny rushed over to the man but he shoved her away.

'I'm… I'm… fine,' he said. 'I'm starving though. You got any food? Any ham? Or maybe some sausage? Or beef? Or brains? Anything like that?' The man looked at them, his eyes hungry as he licked his lips.

'Sorry, no. We have nothing like that. There's a corner shop down the road, though. You could try there?' There was something unsettling about the man. Sunny just wanted him to go away as quickly as possible.

'Shop,' the man said blankly before staggering off in the direction Sunny had pointed.

'Infected,' said Ralph, looking worried.

'What?' said Sunny with a note of grumpiness creeping into her always cheery voice. She was feeling overwhelmed by the talk of zombies and missing pets, and meeting the strange man had thrown her.

'He's infected. According to my comics, when a normal human gets attacked by a zombie but manages to not get eaten, so if they get scratched or bitten but get away, they become infected. They become a zombie themselves.'

'Ralph, I expect he's had a rough night or something. I'm not sure we can assume that everyone who acts a bit strangely is a zombie now.'

Ralph shrugged. 'Maybe, but we need to make sure we've got some protection before we look for these pets. Even if it's only Luca that's a zombie, we don't want to run into him unprotected, do we? Not now we know he's up to something. I say we head to your lab, get some stuff together we can use and then we investigate. You must have something that'll come in handy.'

'Well, I suppose I could find something.' Sunny said with a modest smile. She didn't say anything but she was pleased that he'd thought of her inventions. He was usually dismissive of them and would hurt her feelings by criticising some minor flaw.

'Ok, well what are we waiting for? Let's hit the lab!' Ralph was feeling quite excited now. He loved getting into Sunny's lab and seeing all the mad inventions she'd been cooking up. She was very secretive about the lab, as she didn't like anyone messing with her prototypes until they were ready. Even Ralph had only been in a handful of times.

'Fine. But touch nothing!' Sunny replied as they both began walking towards her house.

* * *

Sunny's laboratory was at the bottom of her parent's garden behind an out-of-control privet hedge that gave her some privacy from her parents. This bit of the garden was dark and dingy, and nobody ever bothered trying to maintain it. The laboratory had once been an old brick built potting shed, but it had fallen into disuse. Sunny's Dad didn't know the difference between a daffodil and a dandelion and wouldn't have had a clue how to put one into a pot even if he'd owned one. The crumbling shed was once so dingy that spiders came from miles around to lurk there. That was before Sunny made it her own. She'd cleared out the old tools and bits of wood and compost that were left there and shut down spider town. They kept trying to get back in, but Sunny had devised a spider-friendly trap she emptied daily to keep the shed arachnid free. She'd repaired the roof and fixed the little window (using the one-way glass they used in police interview rooms to make sure nobody could spy on her inventions) and she'd wired up the shed, so it could use electricity from the main house. It was a small but very handy laboratory for a blossoming young mind.

'Hurry up,' nagged Ralph as Sunny spun the dials on the padlock that kept the lab secure. 'I want to see what you've got inside.'

'You've been in before, Ralph. And all you did was mock my carrot peeling machine - just because it took off a little too much skin,' said Sunny as she cracked open the door.

'All that was left of the carrots were the stalks! What use is a peeler if it peels the actual vegetable away too?' Ralph said with a laugh.

'It was an early prototype! Anyway, all I'm saying is you need to be more thoughtful before you crack jokes about my hard work. OK?' She glared at him without blinking.

'Ohhhkay…'

'Good. Then you can go in. But look with your eyes Cribbens. Some of this stuff can be dangerous unless you've got the brains to handle it properly.' She pulled open the door and nodded her head to show Ralph he could go inside the lab.

Ralph giggled with glee as he crept inside and just as he'd expected, it was like entering Aladdin's cave. The crucial difference being that where Aladdin's cave had been packed with gold and treasure, Sunny's lab overflowed with weird junk and strange contraptions that looked like she had cobbled together them from various bits of broken electronics. She also had a Bunsen burner in one corner, along with several test tubes filled with brightly coloured liquids.

'What's this?' said Ralph, picking up a little silver foil packet. He opened it up and unfolded an unusual-looking glove that was a very pale green colour.

'That,' she said pointing at the glove with a huge grin on her face. '*That* - is the Crisp Mitt.'

'The what?'

'The Crisp Mitt.' Sunny's eyes lit up as she spoke about her invention. Inventing stuff was her passion, and she couldn't help but get enthusiastic about any of her creations.

'What's the worst thing about eating crisps?' she said.

'I dunno. I suppose you might get prawn cocktail flavour if they were the last ones left in the multipack.' Ralph pulled a face to show the disgust he felt for prawn cocktail crisps.

'Incorrect. No, it's getting all of that grease on your fingers. Prawn cocktail is the king of the crisps, Ralph! Honestly!' she said, sounding exasperated. 'You know what I mean, don't you Ralph? When you reach the bottom of the bag and your fingers are covered in grease and salt. It's horrible. I mean, what do you do with the grease? You can lick your fingers, but it never gets it all off, does it? Of course, you can wash your hands, but you aren't always near a sink.'

'Don't you just wipe them on your jumper?'

Sunny shot Ralph a look of utter disgust and continued as if he'd said nothing. 'The Crisp Mitt comes in a handy foil wrap that attaches to the outside of your crisp packet. When it's time to eat your crisps, you simply pop the Crisp Mitt onto your crisp eating hand and tuck in.'

Sunny put the glove on and held it up for Ralph to inspect. 'Note that it's suitable for both right and left-handers.'

'So, it's a rubber glove?' said Ralph, wondering what the fuss was about.

Sunny gave a crazed cackle that sounded a bit too much like the laugh of a deranged super villain. 'No Ralphie, it is *not* a rubber glove. Far from it, in fact. The Crisp Mitt is biodegradable - do you really think I would invent a glove that could just become litter? Really Ralph? And here is the real genius of the Crisp Mitt Ralphie…' Sunny leaned in close to Ralph, as if sharing an important secret, and whispered into his ear. 'The Crisp Mitt is… one hundred percent… edible!'

Sunny put her mitted fingers into her mouth and began to bite and nibble on the fingertips. She pulled with her teeth and as the glove slid off her hand; she gobbled it all up and chewed on it like a piece of gum. 'U shee,' she said, still chewing on the rubbery mitt before swallowing it with a heavy gulp. 'I make The Crisp Mitt from celery, which I process to my own special formula. Now celery, as I'm sure you know, has *negative calories*, which means while eating the Crisp Mitt you are burning off the calories that you consumed when you ate the crisps, thereby allowing you to *eat more crisps*. The crisp companies are going to love this. Stick one of these babies on the side of every bag and people will buy twice as many crisps as they ever did before. They won't even have to worry about eating unhealthy food. The

Crisp Mitt is going to be my ticket to the inventing hall of fame.'

'Yes,' said Ralph, looking bewildered and slightly scared. 'Nobody likes celery though, do they?'

'Well, if they don't, then they can throw the mitt away and just use it to keep their fingers clean so no problem.'

'I guess,' said Ralph. 'Anyway, as ingenious as the Crisp Mitt is, it won't help us take on a hoard of zombies will it? What else have you got here? We need some way to defend ourselves if we get attacked by a zombie.'

Sunny looked around the lab, her brain ticking over while she took in the half-finished contraptions and gizmos she'd been working on. 'Well, I haven't invented anything specifically for dealing with zombies...
There's the Punchatron of course, but that's a one-punch wonder so no use for hordes.'

Ralph nodded, remembering how Sunny had used the Punchatron to save him when Luca had attacked him at the picnic.

'Hmmm. We need to think defensively,' said Sunny. 'I'm not going to rush up to a zombie and hit it with a frying pan, so we have to figure out how we can protect ourselves.'

She started rooting around in a corner, tossing bits of metal and wood around the lab. 'Aha,' she said at last. 'The footy flinger.'

Sunny held up a strange round contraption with several long arms jutting out from a central wheel. An egg whisk that spun the arms when you turned the handle powered it.

'I was working on this for Bernard, so he could practice with six footballs being blasted at him - help him with his reactions.'

'What are we going to do with that thing?' said Ralph, wondering why Sunny had been inventing stuff for Bernard when she'd invented nothing for him. They were supposed to be best friends.

'Well, I've got some bacon in the fridge. I thought we could use that to lure zombies away.'

'Makes sense, I suppose,' said Ralph trying not to sound too grumpy about the footy flinger. 'Do you have anything we could use as armour?'

'Hmm, well…' Sunny started rummaging through a pile of junk. 'I've got loads of these,' she said, holding up what looked like a bag full of old cardboard.

'Egg boxes?! Those won't offer us much protection!' Ralph sounded horrified at the prospect of protecting himself from a zombie with a thin layer of cardboard.

'I don't think it's a bad idea.'

Ralph could virtually see the cogs in Sunny's brain turning as she explained her idea. 'Think about it, Ralph. Egg boxes are light. We could wear them all day without getting tired. If Luca or another zombie came at us, then chances are they'll be trying to bite us. If we made armour out of the egg boxes, then it would leave a gap between the armour and our skin, so even if they bit the armour they'd only get a mouthful of cardboard.'

Ralph had to concede that he could see the sense in her idea. The egg boxes could protect them against zombie bites. They wouldn't hold up against a sustained attack, but what would? And they might give enough protection for them to escape in a pinch.

He nodded. 'You're right,' he said with a grin. 'I knew you'd think of something.'

Sunny beamed at the compliment. She'd expected Ralph to pooh-pooh the idea. 'Great!' she said. 'Let's get to work making them into armour.'

'Just show me what to do.' said Ralph.

* * *

Ralph and Sunny hurried through the park, eyes darting around, checking for danger. Although Ralph had almost convinced Sunny and indeed, himself, that Luca was a pet-eating zombie, they still only had circumstantial evidence so had decided not to wear the egg box armour right away. If you were going to decide to wear egg box armour out in public, you had to be one hundred percent certain that there was imminent danger of a zombie attack.

They'd packed the armour into a large hiking backpack that belonged to Sunny's dad. He'd once trekked across the Himalayas as a young man, but had left the pack in a cupboard for years. Sunny was pretty sure he wouldn't notice that it had gone. The pack was so large that Ralph, who was carrying it, looked like one of those Egyptian dung beetles that push the giant balls of camel poo about with their back legs. Luckily, despite its size, it was still quite light as it contained only egg boxes, a packet of ham and the Footy Flinger.

'Are you sure we shouldn't put the armour on, Ralphie?' said Sunny. She sounded a little breathless as they puffed across the field. 'I mean, you were the one who said we needed protection and now you want to carry it around in a bag.'

'This park is a prime hangout for Breezeblock and his idiot friends. You know as well as I do they would never let us live this down. If you're happy to go skipping about wearing nothing but a set of egg boxes, go right ahead. I'm going to take my chances until we spot an actual zombie.' Ralph had weighed up the options and decided that if the choice was death by zombie or living through the humiliation of being known as Egg Box Boy or the Cardboard Kid for the rest of his school days, he would have to choose death.

They stopped to catch their breath, and Sunny examined the map again. She'd worked out an approximate direction in which whoever or whatever was taking the pets was likely to have headed.

'I think we need to head through those trees up there,' she said, pointing with her pencil to a line of trees in the distance. 'Jerry the Rottweiler from Randall Row went missing around here, and all the squirrels from those trees vanished a day later. We're on the trail, Ralphie. Like a couple of bloodhounds. I can almost smell our quarry.'

'I think that might just be the egg boxes,' Ralph said dryly. He agreed heading for the trees was a good plan. There'd be signs of a struggle if something had eaten the squirrels. The area was always muddy where the trees stopped the sunlight from reaching the ground so there should be tracks.

A chilling silence rested over the park. On a warm, dry day the park should have been packed with people but today the place was empty.

They hurried across the wide grassy field that made up the bulk of the park and scrambled up the banking to the copse of trees.

Although the patch of trees was small and bordered onto a well-used park, the copse was old woodland and as soon as you got between the trees it became thick and dark. Under normal circumstances, you'd see birds in the branches and squirrels scurrying about, even spotting the odd fox was not unusual, but today there was nothing but spooky silence in the shade of the old oaks and beech trees.

'I don't like this Ralph,' said Sunny as they found a narrow path through the trees. 'It's too quiet.'

'Yeah, something doesn't seem right,' Ralph agreed. 'Maybe we should put the armour on?'

Sunny nodded, and they hurried along the path until they found an open area where Ralph could put the pack down and they could get the anti-zombie gear they'd made out. Ralph had been in this clearing before and he remembered seeing birds flitting in and out of the trees and squirrels dancing between the branches. Today there was nothing. It was spooky. The two of them emptied the bag onto the floor and started to armour up. They'd made helmets, neck guards, and body armour, as well as bracers to protect their arms. They left their legs unarmoured as they'd figured that if they met any zombies, their legs were the part of their bodies least likely to get bitten.

Ralph helped Sunny to pull on her body armour and repacked the rest of their stuff into the backpack.

'What is that awful smell?' Sunny asked as Ralph tried to line up her helmet. 'What have you been eating? It smells like rotten meat!'

Ralph sniffed the air. 'Well, it smells like…' A shadow moved in the trees behind Sunny. As his eyes moved to focus on it, a figure lunged up and burst from the thick bushes.

'Sunny look out!' Ralph cried, dropping the footy flinger which he'd been about to stuff into the backpack. Sunny turned and backed away as the grasping hands almost closed around her throat. The thing resembled a man, but its eyes were glazed and blank. Its mouth hung open with the lips drawn back in a frozen snarl. It wore a dark blue business suit and red tie, but the clothes were ripped and dirty, like it had been wandering in the woods for days. Greasy hair hung limp over its twisted face.

'Run!' shouted Ralph.

They took off through the trees like startled rabbits. Branches whipped at their faces and brambles tugged at their clothes and scratched at exposed skin. Ralph's foot caught on a root and he tumbled forward, almost cracking his head on a tree. As Sunny hauled him to his feet, he glanced back and saw the creature stumbling after them.

They were up and running again. As they leapt over a small stream, they could see daylight on the other side of the trees. Just one more dash up the slope and they'd be away. The trees were wider apart here, and as they made their way up the hill the ground was loose with fallen leaves and pine needles. They needed to scramble on all fours to make progress, and a glance behind them told them the strange man was gaining on them. Ralph felt dizzy, and his lungs burned. Sunny was breathing hard now, and her face flushed with exhaustion.

'Come on Ralph!' she cried, but as she did, her footing gave way and she slid into the grasping fingers below.

Ralph shot out an arm and Sunny caught it as she slipped past. Between them, they pulled Sunny free and scrambled up the slope before they toppled through the trees onto the grass on the other side.

Ralph tried to stand but something caught his ankle and he looked down to see a bony hand grabbing at his foot. He turned and tried to pull free by scooting away on his bottom, but it held him fast. He looked at Sunny for help but it had her too. *We're done for*, Ralph thought.

The thing leaned towards them, a wicked hungry grin on its face. It opened its mouth to bite at Ralph's leg, but before it could close its jaws, something large and heavy barrelled into it from the side and sent it crashing back down the slope.

'What's all this then?' shouted the man who'd sent the creature flying. 'Messin' with kiddies! You should be ashamed of yourself!' he bellowed after the man-thing in the suit, who seemed to have disappeared for now.

'Thank you! Oh, thank you!' Sunny cried. 'He would have killed us!'

'Oh yes, I know, blooming zombies!' boomed the man. 'Third one I've had to chase off today!'

Ralph looked at the bear of a man standing beside him. 'You think he was a zombie?' Ralph said to him. It shocked Ralph to hear someone else say the 'Z' word. He'd been wondering whether it was his imagination all along.

'Of course! I know what a zombie looks like,' the man said, as if they were implying he'd be an idiot if he didn't.

He had a lilting musical voice Ralph recognised as a Welsh accent thanks to the holiday to Tenby he'd been on last year.

'Slobbering lips, dead eyes, stink of rotting meat. You'd have to be born yesterday to not know a zombie when you see one,' said the man.

He was a tall older gentleman, around fifty if Ralph was any judge of these things (which he wasn't but by chance he happened to be close this time). He had the sort of round pot belly that older men can get if they enjoy their beer a bit too much. His hair was dark but peppered with flecks of grey and he was bald on top (though for some reason he had kept it longer on the sides). He also had thick bristly sideburns that adorned his cheeks like a couple of sleeping poodles. He wore an old red and black tracksuit it looked like he'd outgrown thanks to his expanding girth.

The man held out his hand for Ralph and Sunny to shake.

'JC Williams-Davies at your service.'

'Thank you, Mr Williams-Davies,' said Sunny.

'No need to thank me boys, it was a pleasure. I haven't had the chance to hit someone with a proper tackle in years. I coach the under 12's see, so don't get the chance to get properly stuck in. And please, call me JC.'

'Thanks JC,' said Sunny. 'And by the way, I'm a girl not a boy.'

She couldn't believe he hadn't noticed given her explosion of curly blonde hair and the green flowery dress she was wearing. She wasn't a *girly* girl, but she'd never been mistaken for a boy.

'That's alright, I won't hold it against you. We are very much an equal opportunities sport.'

Now that they'd shaken off the delirium of the chase through the woods, Ralph and Sunny realised they had come up on the sports pitches that bordered the woodland on the opposite side to the park.

'You mean rugby?' questioned Sunny.

'Course I do. You can't tackle like that in football, can you? Bunch of prancing primadonnas! Rolling around on the floor if you as much as look at them funny they are. So yes, I mean rugby.'

'What's that cardboard you've got on you all about then?' said JC, seeming to notice the egg box armour that covered the two children for the first time.

'It's for protection,' said Sunny, she always got defensive about her theories. 'The egg boxes are raised off the skin, so if the zombies bite through them their teeth don't touch your skin.'

'Not a bad idea to be fair,' JC gave an appreciative nod. 'But if you ask me, attack is the best form of defence. If you've got a few minutes, I can show you a few moves. It doesn't look like anyone's coming to training today, so I've got time.'

Ralph and Sunny looked at each other. Ralph gave a non-committal shrug of his shoulders, but after her experience with the zombie, Sunny wanted to learn anything that might give them an edge.

'We'd love to,' Sunny said.

'Lovely,' said JC with a grin. 'I know just the thing to practice on!'

He disappeared away through the trees and down the slope before re-emerging a few minutes later, dragging the zombie that had attacked them. As Ralph and Sunny watched in horror, JC crammed an old rugby sock into its mouth before taping it up with some bandage. He then took the rest of the bandage and tied its hand together behind its back.

'You can't beat a moving target, I always say. Who wants to go first?'

'What do you expect us to do with that?' Ralph said, gesturing at the zombie stumbling around on the grass.

'Tackle it, of course!' said JC with a grin. He was getting into it now, delighted he'd got to do some coaching after all. 'Now watch me closely. You'll be doing this next and I won't be showing you again.'

JC moved over to the zombie and spun the startled monster around to face the two children.

'This here is your opponent,' he said, gesturing at the creature.

Ralph glanced over at Sunny and rolled his eyes. She tried to suppress a giggle as JC continued his lecture.

'His most dangerous weapons,' JC continued, 'are his teeth, here,' he pointed with a stick, shoving it right at the zombie's gnashing mouth. 'So, to give yourself the best chance possible of avoiding these weapons, you need to go in low. Aim to take the zombie around the waist if possible, make the contact with your shoulder before you power through using your legs and you will knock him to the ground no matter how big he is. Observe.'

JC took two quick steps back and then another slower one before shooting forward with a sudden burst of speed. He was much taller than the zombie, so had to duck low before launching himself headlong at the thing. His shoulder hit the astonished creature hard in the stomach and he sent it spinning backwards to lay sprawling on the grass. JC popped up at once with an enormous smile on his face.

'There you go! Easy! Right, come on boys. You can have the first go,' he pointed at Ralph.

'I think Sunny would be better—' Ralph started.

'Don't be daft, anyone can do it!' cut in JC. He put a comforting hand on Ralph's shoulder. 'Listen to me, sunshine. I know you think you're a bit on the skinny side for rugby, but it don't matter how big someone is, if you hit them with one of those they're going over. Believe me!'

Ralph gave a tentative nod. JC's argument hadn't quite convinced him, but he was almost as worried about what JC would do if he refused to try the tackle as he was about the zombie. It *was* tied and gagged, so he figured he might as well give it a go.

'OK, OK, let's do it.' Ralph was eager to get on with it, mainly so he could get his go over and done with and relax while Sunny took her turn.

JC dragged the still dazed zombie back to its feet.

'Stay there now, boy,' he told it cheerfully, patting it on its ragged shoulder.

'Go on then, boy… What was your name again?'

'Ralph,' said Ralph.

'And I'm Sunny,' added Sunny.

'Great stuff. Get stuck in, Ralph.'

JC clapped his hands, which Ralph assumed was a gesture for this madness to begin. What was he thinking? Choosing to attack a zombie with his bare hands couldn't be a good idea, could it?

'Go on, Ralphie! You can do it!' Sunny shouted.

Ralph gritted his teeth and charged at the zombie. He leaped at it and caught it in a firm grip around the waist. It wobbled a bit but didn't go down. The creature looked at him, cold eyes seeming to stare into his soul. Ralph felt panic rising as it recovered from the initial shock and began to use its weight to gain the advantage.

'Drive! Drive with your legs!' JC bellowed. 'You've forgotten to do the most important part! You need to get those leg muscles working and drive him over. Come on, boy!'

Ralph started pumping his legs like a deranged grape treader. He wasn't sure whether what he was doing was working or whether it was just that the zombie was slipping on the muddy ground, but somehow the thing tumbled backward and crashed to the floor with Ralph slamming down on top of it.

The impact must have forced the air from the creature's mouth as the sock JC had taped there popped up into the air. The zombie bared its teeth and lunged at Ralph, who darted clear before JC rammed the sock back into its mouth.

'Wow Ralph, you showed him who's the boss around here. I didn't know you had that sort of power in you!' Sunny gave Ralph a cheeky wink at Ralph and flexed her biceps. Ralph gave her a wary look, unsure if he was being mocked.

'Well done, boy. Dai iawn. You got him down and that's the main thing. Well, that and him not tearing chunks out of you,' said JC in his cheerful Welsh accent. 'Right, your turn now, Sunny boy.'

'I've already told you I'm a girl!' Sunny replied, stamping her foot.

'And I told you that's fine...' JC started, but something had caught his eye behind Sunny.

Across the playing field a group of around fifteen children were making their way towards them, but something was wrong with the way they moved. Instead of running, skipping and walking as children tended to do, they shambled with a strange staggering gait. Some of them had their arms outstretched, and they were moaning something that Ralph couldn't quite make out.

'Looks like my team has turned up after all,' said JC, sounding almost regretful. 'You two had better run along. They'll think I'm moonlighting training another side. They're keen today as well - I can hear them all shouting how they wants to "trains".'

'I don't think they're shouting about that,' said Sunny.

'Go on, boys, off you go now before they get here, they'll get awful jealous if they see me coaching someone else,' he gestured for them to move away. 'Go on,' he added, more grimly this time. 'And remember what I told you about driving with your legs.'

With that, he jogged off towards the team at the far end of the field.

'Come on, we'd better go,' said Ralph.

'But those are zombies!' said Sunny. 'We can't just...'

'We can. We must. JC knows what they are as well as we do. There are too many and he'd have to worry about us *and* watch his own back,' replied Ralph. 'He'll be fine. You know he can handle himself.'

85

Ralph was not so sure about this. He was certain JC could handle a couple of zombies, but fifteen might be too many for him, even if they were half his size.

His argument convinced Sunny, though, and she nodded. The zombie rugby players were getting closer, and they needed to get away.

Pulling Sunny with him, Ralph took off in the opposite direction to which the zombies were coming, not daring to look back at JC.

7

Knock, Knock. Who's Scared?

Ralph and Sunny sprinted away from the playing fields through a patch of scrub land, down an alleyway and onto a street lined with large expensive mansions. The houses each had tall, neatly trimmed hedges that gave the wealthy owners privacy from passers-by. The pair kept running until they were halfway up the road when Ralph pulled up, grabbing Sunny by the shoulder to stop her.

'Stop. Stop. I can't go on!'

Sunny tutted in disapproval. 'Ralph, we've only just jogged down the street. I can still hear JC shouting at his team. You *really* need to work on your stamina.'

'I have weak lungs!' Ralph wheezed. 'And anyway, we can't run everywhere. There could be zombies around any corner so no point tiring ourselves out.'

Sunny nodded. 'We need to decide what to do now. There's no point trying to find more evidence. It's obvious people are turning into zombies, so we need to just report it to the police and let them deal with it.'

'What if they don't believe us?' said Ralph between gasps for air as he struggled to get his breath back.

'JC knew about the zombies, so I doubt we'd be the only ones who reported it,' said Sunny. 'If enough people told them I'm sure they'd do something. If only this had happened next month, I could have just called them - Dad says I can have a mobile phone for my birthday.'

'Who are you gonna call? Fat chance I'll get a phone until I can afford to buy my own!' snorted Ralph.

'Believe it or not, Ralph, there are other people I might want to call. Though, as it happens, the main reason I want it is so I can build mobile functionality into some of my inventions. Not that it's any of your business!' Sunny snapped. 'Do you really think your Dad wouldn't get you a phone? Nearly everyone gets one by the end of year 7, even if it's just an old one,' she added, giving Ralph a sympathetic half-smile.

'You know what Dad and Imelda are like. They'd start banging on about how they never had phones in their day and how it would toughen me up to get trapped in a burning building with no way of calling for help.'

'Don't be so dramatic, Ralph!'

'I'm not. This is all their fault, you know.'

'What is?' Sunny asked, puzzled.

'This.' Ralph raised his arms wide and spun half around. 'Everything. The zombies. If they hadn't ordered a kid from some dodgy website just because I didn't match their expectations, none of this would have happened.'

'But they didn't know Luca was going to turn out to be a monster, Ralph.' Sunny, pushed her bushy yellow hair away from her face. 'They just wanted another child. Imelda doesn't have any other kids, so it's not that strange she wants to adopt, is it? You could argue they did a really good thing, taking on a poor kid who's lost his parents and bringing him into their home.'

'Yes, that's fine,' said Ralph but he wasn't going to let this go. 'My point is they only did it because I'm not up to scratch as far they're concerned. I can't even assemble a flat packed cardboard box - let alone landscape a garden! I'm not the son they wanted, so they thought they could order in another one.'

'Not everything is always about you, Ralph. There are plenty of other reasons for them to want another child.'

'Cheap manual labour?!' said Ralph sarcastically.

'Maybe they thought it would be nice for you to have some company?'

Ralph gave an ironic chuckle. 'Maybe. Anyway, look, we can't just hang around here it's too exposed. The police station isn't far, so maybe you should jog there? You could give me a piggyback.'

'Ralphie, of course I'll give you a piggyback!' Sunny said with glee. 'As long as you don't mind if I drop you in the river while we're crossing the bridge, of course,' she added with menace. 'Wouldn't it make more sense to knock on somebody's doors and get one of them to call the police for us?'

'I guess so,' said Ralph. 'I've never been in one of these posh houses. The kids round here all go to the grammar school over in Offelton.'

They started walking up the nearest drive, which cut through a tall thick hedge. They could make out the roof of the enormous detached property it hid, so they knew there was a house behind it somewhere. Light-brown gravel that crunched under Ralph's feet covered the driveway as they made their way towards the house. Once they were past the hedge, they could see the enormous front garden along with the stunning mansion to which it belonged.

'We'll probably have to get past the butler first,' Ralph joked.

Ralph found approaching the big house intimidating. He couldn't shake the feeling that they didn't belong, and they were trespassing somewhere they shouldn't be. Ralph expected to get told to clear off as soon as he rang the doorbell, but it was worth a try. He'd already decided that if the owners answered he would not mention zombies, or they'd have him carted off to the looney bin faster than they could say how terribly cross they were that a pair of horrid urchins were loitering on their doorstep.

The house didn't have a bell, but a heavy brass door knocker that they needed to lift and slam down. Sunny tried it first, lifting the knocker and dropping it to give a very polite little 'tap'. They stood on the doorstep for a few moments, waiting politely for a response.

'You know Sunny, I've always wanted to give one of those big door knockers a proper go…' Ralph and Sunny looked at each other and giggled. Together they took hold of the knocker and lifted it up high before slamming it three times into the metal knocking plate. The noise cracked like cannon fire and echoed up and down the street.

Nobody came to answer the door. In fact, as their laughter subsided in the quiet that followed, Ralph and Sunny became aware of how spooky the silence was. No dogs barked, or babies cried, and no cars passed on the road outside.

'Let's try a couple more houses,' said Sunny, but Ralph could tell the eerie silence had spooked her from the way she kept chewing her lip.

They moved on, calling at the next two houses on the street. Both had cars parked on the driveways so should have been good options, but when they rang the bells, again there was no response. The third house they tried was another with a door knocker. They gave it a mighty bang, but there was no giggling this time.

'Something is not right here. The place is like a ghost town. Where is everyone?' said Sunny.

'Let's give it one more knock, then we go on to the police station,' said Ralph. He raised the knocker but as he tried to slam it again, something grabbed his arm from behind.

Ralph let out a terrified squeal and shrank to the floor, cowering. He covered his head with his arms, trying to protect himself against the zombie attack.

'Are you two out of your minds?' said a tall boy with curly afro hair.

'Hello,' said Sunny with a quizzical smile. 'Who are you?'

'And what are you doing sneaking up on people like that?' Ralph added as he picked himself up off the floor.

'I'm sneaking because I'm trying to be quiet. You should try it sometime,' the boy hissed. 'And my name is Benjamin.'

'I'm Sunny and he's Ralph. Don't mind him. He's been having a bad day, and you gave him a bit of a fright,' Sunny offered Benjamin her hand to shake.

'Haven't we all?' said Benjamin, accepting Sunny's handshake before offering his hand to Ralph. 'Sorry about that, Ralph. I didn't mean to give you a scare, but banging on those big door knockers is not a good idea right now.'

'It's fine. Don't worry about it,' said Ralph, who had recovered at least some of his cool. 'Is this your house, Benjamin?'

'Mine is the one over there,' Benjamin replied, pointing across the street to the largest of all the enormous houses.

The boy's clothes were smart, brown chinos and a red and black checked shirt. He even wore polished shoes, which Ralph found baffling. He would never have considered wearing anything other than trainers if it wasn't a school day. The boy was dressed like he was going to church or a family wedding.

Despite his spiffing attire, the boy looked untidy. His shirt was untucked, and he had patches of mud on his trousers. His hair was frizzy and unkempt.

'Have you noticed how quiet it is?' Benjamin said in a low voice.

'Yes, we were just saying—' Sunny began.

'That's because there's nobody here,' said Benjamin.

'Right,' said Ralph.

He looked at Sunny and tried to read whether she thought the boy was as crazy as he did.

'I mean, I went out last night to my chess club. And when I came back, everyone had vanished. I couldn't get into my house. My family aren't the sorts to go wandering off. They don't just disappear without letting me know. I tried all the neighbours' houses, but it was the same thing. They've all gone. I didn't even have a key, so I ended up sleeping in the shed.'

'Oh, you poor thing. But why haven't you gone to the police?' said Sunny, putting a sympathetic arm around him.

'I was going to. I started walking towards the police station. But… when I got down near that new restaurant, *Gumbo Jumbo*, there were these people in the road. They looked like normal people, but they were acting seriously weird. Shuffling around, mumbling… most of them had their arms stretched out in front of them like they were trying to grab something. I got scared, so I ran back here and hid in the shed.'

'You did the right thing,' said Ralph.

'I've seen a few of them around today too. That's why I didn't want you to bang on the door knockers. There's nobody in anyway,' said Benjamin.

'Well, thanks for stopping us. I just hope we won't have a host of zombies arriving after we banged on the other door,' Ralph replied.

'Zombies? Yeah, I thought they seemed like zombies too. But zombies aren't real, are they?' asked Benjamin, his eyes wide.

'Well actually, voodoo witch doctors used to put people into a zombie-like state so it's not beyond the realm of possibility,' said Ralph. 'I suppose it's quite an unusual occurrence in a small British town though,' he admitted. 'The thing is, people are definitely behaving in what you'd have to say is a zombie-like manner, so for the sake of simplicity we'll call them zombies.'

'Whatever they are and whatever caused this, we need to tell someone as soon as possible,' Sunny said. 'We aren't far from the Police Station, so we should just—'

'No way,' Benjamin cut in. 'No way. *We are not* going there. I told you what it was like. If you saw those people—those *zombies*—you wouldn't go either. They felt... dangerous.'

'We have seen them,' said Ralph. 'We know about them too. That's why it's so important we get to the Police Station. Someone needs to let them know.'

'They must already know. The zombie people were all over the road!'

'What do you want to do? Spend another night in the shed? I thought you wanted to find your family? The houses are all locked up so you can't wait for someone to come and find you. It's not safe,' Ralph challenged before a look from Sunny quieted him.

Benjamin hung his head, wiping away the tears that were welling in his eyes.

'It's ok Benji,' Sunny soothed. 'You can stick with us now. Let's just look. If it's too dangerous, then we'll head back and have a rethink.'

Benjamin nodded and wiped away some snot that had dripped out of his nose. 'Benji? That sounds like a dog's name,' he whimpered.

'Well that's ok. I like dogs, so take it as a compliment.'

'She does it to everyone.' Ralph added.

'He's Ralph so I call him Ralphie, You're Benjamin so I'm going to call you Benji. Obviously, I'm Sunny so you can continue to call me Sunny.'

'I can think of a few other names we could call you,' Ralph sniggered.

Benjamin chuckled, and Ralph was glad to see the newcomer was calming down about the prospect of heading towards the Police Station. It worried Ralph he might have another meltdown, but they *had* to get there. They could have headed back Ralph's house and called from his Mum and Dad's phone, but that was the other side of town. It made sense to go to the Police Station.

Sunny shot Ralph a glare, but he could tell she didn't mean it and was just as glad as he was that Benjamin seemed to feel a bit better.

'Okay, before we go I think we ought to armour up,' Sunny said. 'Ralph, open the pack and we'll share out the kit.'

'You have armour? Oh, that's brilliant. That should make things safer,' said Benjamin, visibly relaxing.

Ralph hefted the large pack off his back. Despite the light boxes inside, it was feeling like a burden. He opened it and pulled out the individual pieces of armour that they'd made in Sunny's lab and stacked them up on the porch of the house outside which they were standing.

'Hold on… Aren't those egg boxes? Are you actually thinking we can protect ourselves with a load of old egg boxes?'

'Don't worry, we've got this figured out. The bumps stop the zombies from biting through to your skin and they're lightweight. It's up to you but we'll be wearing them,' said Ralph as he started suiting up in his protective cardboard coverings.

Benjamin looked dubious, but he covered himself in the boxes anyway. Sunny and Ralph hadn't planned on giving anyone else any of the armour but they'd made a few back-up pieces and between them they were pretty much covered.

'You two look ridiculous,' joked Benjamin.

'That's funny because it suits you Benji,' retorted Sunny, drawing a laugh from Benjamin for the first time.

Ralph slung the now empty backpack over his shoulder, 'Okay, are we ready?' he said.

The others both looked serious as they nodded their heads and the three of them set out towards town.

8
Inspector Corpse

The streets were empty as the children made their way towards the town centre and the police station. It was the quiet that Ralph found the most disturbing. There was no birdsong and no traffic on the roads. It made the familiar streets of Great Merritt feel unsettling and scary. Every bush and every corner hid a potential zombie ambush and as they got closer to town, they grew more and more jumpy.

As the long avenue into town finally opened up into the main High Street, the town centre was as empty as the streets that surrounded it.

'The police station is over there,' said Benjamin, pointing at a large grey building with a blue sign about a hundred metres ahead of them.

'OK, let's go. Keep your eyes peeled, everyone,' said Ralph as he headed out onto the road.

They kept a steady, cautious pace as they made their way up the road past the *Bunch of Chives*—the greengrocer that was also a florist—and past the gumbo restaurant that everyone was raving about.

They crossed the road to the police station and darted inside, slamming the door behind them.

It was an old small-town station. The reception area had peeling paint on the walls and boards filled with posters encouraging visitors to leave their lights on when they left the house and join their neighbourhood watch. There was a front desk which Ralph thought would be surrounded by bulletproof glass, but was actually a normal reception desk similar to one you might find in a hairdresser's or a hotel. Nobody was at the desk, but you could ring a bell to let the sergeant know you were waiting.

Sunny started banging on the bell and shouting for the sergeant. 'Hello? Hello?! We have quite an important situation going on if you haven't already noticed! Can someone come and see us, please?'

'Maybe they're in a meeting or something? We should just wait here until someone comes down,' said Benjamin.

Ralph though, was looking at the desk. It had a section that lifted up with a little half-door underneath, so you could open the desk to get behind it. Ralph flipped the top section over, opened the door and walked behind the desk.

'What are you doing?' said Benjamin in horror. 'You'll get us all arrested.'

Ralph ignored him and made his way to the inner door the police officers must have used to get inside the body of the station. 'It's open,' he said.

'You can't be serious!' said Benjamin. 'Sunny, tell him!'

'This is an extraordinary situation. I'm sure they wouldn't mind this once,' Sunny replied, following Ralph behind the sergeant's desk.

Benjamin groaned. 'Oooh no. I've fallen in with a bad crowd. Mum's gonna kill me when she finds out about this. She always warned me about falling in with the wrong sorts. They leave me alone for one day and it's already happened. I'm sorry Mum, I'll be a good boy from now on,' he muttered to himself.

He looked around and realised that the others had already gone in without him. 'Hey you guys! Wait for me!'

The door opened onto a corridor with several smaller rooms coming off it. The smaller rooms were set up for dealing with various crimes committed in the Great Merritt area, with photos and maps all over the walls.

'Hello? Hello?!' shouted Sunny. 'We need a police officer. There's been an incident you might want to know about!'

To Benjamin's dismay, Ralph wandered into one of the side rooms. He didn't think anyone was in there; he was just being nosy now, and he'd spotted something that looked familiar.

Ralph stared up at a pin board filled with printouts of grey CCTV images.

'Sunny - come and look at this.'

'What is it?' said Benjamin as Sunny came up behind the boys and peered over their shoulders.

'Is that... is that *Luca*?' she said.

'It certainly looks like him,' agreed Ralph. 'It's hard to be sure, though. The photo is too grainy.'

'This one here,' Sunny pointed to another photo. 'It's the man who chased us in the woods earlier.'

'And these people were in the crowd on the High Street yesterday.' Benjamin added, squinting at another blurry photograph.

Ralph noticed a map of Great Merritt on the wall. 'Look, they've drawn a big circle around most of the town. They definitely know about the zombies.'

The others nodded in agreement.

'Let's go upstairs. The police officers must be up there,' said Benjamin.

The three children moved back out onto the corridor and followed it until they reached an atrium with a wide curved staircase that led up to offices on the floor above, and down to a basement. It seemed unlikely the police would have congregated in the basement, so they headed up.

Upstairs the offices were larger and filled with desks with computers perched on top, but there weren't any more people about. One room looked like people had been there recently as they'd left a pile of takeaway containers lying around on the desk.

'Okay, this is worrying. How can there be no police officers in the entire police station? Where is everyone?' Ralph muttered.

'Maybe they were called away to an emergency or something,' replied Sunny.

'There's still the basement,' said Benjamin. 'I know it's a bit of a longshot they'll be down there, but it's worth a look.'

'Good point, Benji,' agreed Sunny. 'Let's take a look.'

They doubled back and headed down the stairs, bypassing the ground floor and heading straight down to the basement. The stairs didn't open directly onto the corridor like they did on the other floors. Instead, there was a heavy metal door that they had to pull open. The door gave a loud creak as they pulled it back, the noise echoing around the basement.

'Hello?' a voice called, from the far end of the dark basement.

'There's someone here!' Sunny chirped, her face lighting up. 'Hello!' she shouted.

Laughing with relief they moved forward into the darkness causing the automatic lights to pop on.

'Where are they?' said Benjamin. 'I still can't see anyone.'

'Hello - who said that?' called Ralph.

'Over 'ere,' said the voice.

The basement was another corridor, this time filled with heavy steel doors like the one they'd just come through. One was open and they could see it was a small kitchen with a fridge and a kettle. The children were so relieved to hear the voice they pelted down the corridor to the final door, the one from which the voice was emanating.

Ralph pulled at the door, but it wouldn't open.

'It's locked,' said the voice. 'You gotta slide the bolt back.'

Ralph reached for the bolt but before he could close his fingers around it, Sunny and Benjamin grabbed him and yanked him away from the door.

He spun ready to snap at them, but as he opened his mouth, he realised where they were.

'Ralph, that man is a prisoner - I'm not sure it's such a good idea to be talking to him, let alone opening his cell,' said Benjamin.

'C'mon kids.' said the prisoner. 'Have a little heart. The Old Bill has left me down here for hours. They've not even gave me my breakfast yet. Not even a cup of tea!'

'He could be a murderer or anything,' said Sunny.

'Nah, nah. You've got me wrong, little lady. I'm no murderer, would they lock me up 'ere if I was? They'd have carted me off to the big cop shop up in the city. I'm just a err, trespasser. Yeah, I took a short-cut through a warehouse and someone called the boys in blue. It was all a big misunderstanding.'

'He's a thief,' said Benjamin, who'd picked up a police record book. 'Looks like he got caught loading boxes of mobile phones into a van at this warehouse. He wasn't "trespassing".'

'Like I say, it was a misunderstanding. And anyway, I ain't dangerous am I? I might be a wrong 'un but I wouldn't hurt a couple of kiddies, would I? 'Specially not in the middle of the cop shop,' pleaded the man.

'We can't trust him,' said Benjamin.

'Definitely not,' agreed Sunny.

'How long since you saw a policeman?' Ralph asked through the door.

'Open the door and I'll tell you,' the man said. 'At least open the inspection slot, so you can look at me. Then you'll see me honest face and want to let me out straight away.'

Ralph didn't need to see the man's face to know he was smiling when he spoke. He pulled the sliding cover open and peered in through the slot.

''ello kids,' said the man. He was younger than he sounded. He looked to be in his mid-twenties with a mop of shoulder length black hair. He wore a collared black t-shirt, black motorcycle boots, and dark blue jeans.

'Name's Guy. Now, are you kids going to let me out of 'ere or what? I know there're no coppers 'ere cos I've not heard anyone about in hours. They would have been in to give me a bit of grub. You gotta do something else I'll starve... are those *egg boxes* you've got stuck all over you?'

Ignoring the question about the egg boxes, Sunny spun on her heels and headed off down the corridor before disappearing into the little police kitchen. She re-emerged a few moments later carrying a cheese sandwich and a cup of water.

'Here you go then Guy,' she said, handing him the sandwich. 'We couldn't live with ourselves if we let you starve but I'm afraid we aren't about to let a hardened criminal out of jail just because he's had to skip breakfast.'

'Fair enough,' replied Guy, taking the sandwich with a toothy grin. 'So, what are you kids doing here, anyway? And where the 'ell 'ave all the coppers gone? What is it, World War Three out there?'

'Not quite, but it looks like it might be a zombie apocalypse,' said Ralph as they headed back upstairs.

Guy hooted with laughter. 'Good one, kid. Good one. Cheers for the sarnie. Much appreciated!'

Just then, a loud ringing sound came from upstairs.

'The bell from the sergeant's desk!' said Sunny. 'There must be someone up there.'

'Well, it won't be a police officer. Why would they ring their own bell?' Ralph asked.

'It doesn't matter. It'll be nice to see an actual adult who is not a flesh-eating zombie,' answered Benjamin. 'Or a criminal,' he added, glancing over his shoulder at Guy, who had his face pressed up against the slot in his cell door.

They ran up the stairs and down the hallway, back to the door into the Reception area. They opened the door and found to their surprise that people packed the Reception.

Ralph wondered what must have brought everyone here at the same time. He supposed people must have just realised what was going on with the zombies.

Ralph caught the eye of someone at the front of the crowd and his stomach turned a somersault as he realised he was staring into a pair of cold, dead eyes he recognised all too well.

'Luca!' he sputtered.

'Brrraiinns,' replied Luca, as the others all joined in with his baleful cry. 'Brrraiinns,' they all groaned. 'Brrraiinns.'

The Reception area wasn't full of people as they'd first thought; the place was jam-packed with moaning zombies. Ralph even noticed a couple of police zombies, still wearing their uniforms and helmets.

Sunny had started opening the desk door when the groans of the zombies startled her into looking up. She jumped back in horror as a man in a ragged black suit reached across the desk, trying to grab her as she pulled away.

'They want to eat our brains!' shrieked Benjamin in terror as he cowered back against the wall.

'Ohhhh,' said Ralph to Sunny. 'Brains! Of course! That makes sense now. Now that I know he's saying brains it seems so obvious,' he mused.

'What are you talking about?' Benjamin growled, still pressing himself against the far wall.

'Nevermind,' said Ralph. 'Just ruuuuuun!'

They bolted for the door back into the station. The three of them squeezing through the opening together before slamming it shut behind them.

'We need to get out of here! Do you think there's a back door?' said Benjamin as they ran down the corridor. 'All the windows have bars on them!'

'We should let Guy out first,' said Ralph.

'Have you lost your mind?' snapped Benjamin in horror. 'Is the horde of zombies not bad enough for you? You want to have a hardened criminal running around as well?'

'You said yourself he's just a thief. That doesn't mean he's going to be some crazy psycho.'

'We should let him out,' Sunny agreed. 'If he's a thief, that should mean he's pretty good at breaking into places, so maybe he'll be useful for breaking us out. And anyway, we can't just leave him locked up. The zombies will gobble him up like I would gobble up a packet of Jaffa Cakes.'

They charged down the stairs into the cells and Ralph slammed back the bolt that was holding Guy's cell door shut.

'Couldn't keep away, eh?' Guy quipped.

Ralph twisted the handle and pulled at the door, trying to yank it open, but it held fast.

'Oh, you'll need the key for that too,' said Guy, pointing at the keyhole. 'Thinking about it, the Custody Officer usually just has that on him.'

'The policeman in reception!' said Ralph. 'He had a bunch of keys tied to his belt!'

'That'll be him,' said Guy, who seemed to find the whole thing amusing. 'Better go and ask him for them. I'm sure he won't mind handing them over.'

'No way am I going back up there,' said Benjamin.

'It's too dangerous,' agreed Sunny. 'We should just hide out here until they've gone.'

A loud banging came from upstairs as the zombies reached the door and started clawing and pounding at it.

'We need to get it now or it will be too late. If they find us here we're trapped,' said Ralph, his face grim. 'I'm going to go up and try to grab them.'

'Ralphie no!' said Sunny. 'You're not going! Not without me anyway.'

Benjamin gave a loud sigh. 'Fine! I'll come too then,' he said, gritting his teeth.

Ralph nodded, and they headed upstairs. As they approached the door, the banging got louder and they could hear moaning from the other side. The zombies massed outside the door and from the way it was bulging on its hinges it wouldn't be long before they were inside.

Ralph grabbed a broom that he found propped up against a wall and handed it to Benjamin.

'You're the biggest, so we need you on crowd control duty. Sunny, you just open the door. I'm going to take a quick peek so we can figure out where that policeman is. Just open it a crack and then push it shut again straight away.'

Ralph positioned himself next to the door and got ready to peer through the crack. He nodded to Sunny, and she pulled it open a fraction before pushing it shut again at once. In just that instant she could feel the weight of the zombies pressing against the door.

'Did you see him?' she said.

Ralph nodded. 'He's near the front, thankfully. Second one in. I guess he must have some memory of the building from the time before he became a zombie. It makes sense he'd be near the front. Benjamin, there is a short blonde woman wearing sunglasses at the front. Clear her out of the way, so I can get to zombie cop. Just charge her with the broom to knock her back and hold her there. I'll duck underneath and grab the keys off his belt.'

They settled into their positions again and Ralph counted them in.

'Three, two, one... now!' he mouthed silently.

Sunny yanked the door open wide this time, and for a moment the three of them gawked at the seething mass of limbs and vacant faces that swarmed in the reception. There were zombies everywhere. Although they were still recognisable as people, it was clear from the way they moved, their slack jaws and their hideous rotting smell that something was wrong with them. They were something inhuman now. Luca himself wasn't there anymore, or if he was, the crowd had swallowed him up.

The blonde woman in the sunglasses was the first to react. She reared up and lunged at Ralph. Benjamin gave a yell and charged forward with the broom held up in front of him. He caught the woman in the neck, knocking her backwards into the mass of zombies. Benjamin kept the broom outstretched, pinning her in place. Her eyes flashed with rage and she screamed a blood-curdling cry but for the moment she was helpless.

Ralph ducked under the broom and grabbed at the keyring. He yanked and pulled at it, but it refused to come free. The policeman had attached it to his belt loop by a metal keyring.

'Come on, Ralph!' screeched Benjamin. 'I can't hold her much longer. The rest of them are pushing forward.'

Ralph got frantic. *I can't get them*, he thought. *They're stuck fast…* A smaller zombie squeezed out of the crowd and fell on top of him - teeth gnashing and chewing at the egg box padding protecting the back of his neck. *I'm about to be the meat in a zombie sandwich*, he thought as his shaking fingers continued to pull at the key ring. He heard a 'snick' sound, and the ring came free. Benjamin changed his attention from the woman to the smaller zombie, which looked like it had been a teenage girl. He shoved her off Ralph's back and Sunny grabbed Ralph's ankles, dragging him back through the door. As soon as he was through, Benjamin yanked the broom back and threw his weight against the door. The zombies surged forward, and the door bulged again, but the zombies didn't seem to have figured out how the handle worked. He drew the bolt across, securing it behind him.

Ralph lay back on the floor, his heart pounding. 'The keys wouldn't come free! A zombie nearly had me for lunch, but then they just came loose in my hand.'

Sunny held up a pair of scissors and made a few snips in the air.

'I always carry a pair of scissors for emergencies. You never know when they're gonna come in handy.'

'You saved my life Sunny,' said Ralph. 'I don't know how to thank you.'

'I would say you could take me to the cinema but we all needed you to get those keys so I'll let you off this time.'

'That door won't last much longer,' said Benjamin, eyeing the door that was now straining and creaking at the hinges with the weight of zombies pressed against it.

They sprinted back down to the cells.

'Come on then, Guy. Don't make us regret this,' said Ralph when they reached the thief's cell.

'I'll be as good as gold kids. Scouts honour,' grinned Guy.

The keyring had about a dozen different keys on it. Ralph slipped the first one into the lock and tried to turn it but it wouldn't budge. He let out a huff of frustration and tried another. The sound of the banging from upstairs got louder and louder. Sunny and Benjamin glanced at each other, wondering if Ralph was turning the keys properly.

'Do you want me to try, Ralph?' said Sunny just as the cell unlocked with an audible click.

'No thank you,' replied Ralph with a smug grin.

Guy stepped out of his cell with a smile. 'Now then. What's all this nonsense about zombies?' he said.

A booming thump echoed from the hallway upstairs as the door to reception gave way and burst open, sending splinters flying down the corridor.

'I think you're about to find out Guy!' said Sunny, already running for the stairs with Benjamin and Ralph close behind.

Guy looked like he was about to say something, but changed his mind and followed the kids up the stairs.

They burst into the corridor to find the zombies swarming towards them. The creatures were falling over each other to get a taste of their victims. They shambled slowly, but there was a hunger in them that made them terrifying.

'Blimey! You weren't kidding!' gasped Guy. 'Quick, up to next floor.'

They ran for the staircase, but Guy hung back and darted into an office. He re-emerged seconds later dragging a table which he pulled to the stairs before turning it over to use as a barricade.

The four of them sprinted to the furthest upstairs office and slammed the door behind them. Guy picked up a chair and swung it at the window, shattering it in a couple of hits. Looking down, they could see the street was full of zombies too.

'I didn't even know that many people lived in Great Merritt!' wailed Benjamin.

'It's clearer up the road. If we drop to the garage roofs below, we can run over the top of them and make a break for the river at the end of the road,' said Guy.

'It's too high,' said Ralph 'We can't jump to the roofs.'

'It's that or wait here for those things to tear us apart. I'll lower you three down, then jump down after. That kind of drop is bread and butter to me.'

Ralph forced himself to climb out of the window and took Guy's arm. Guy leaned out and lowered him as far as he could reach and then, with a wink, he let go. Ralph was about to scream, but before he could get it out, he was falling. The next thing he knew, he was back on solid ground as he landed heavily and rolled across the rooftop. He looked up to see Sunny dropping next to him with Benjamin close behind. He watched Guy pick up a chair and throw it back into the room. The zombies were right on top of him. Guy turned and hurdled out of the full-length window, landing with a professional-looking roll next to Ralph.

'What are you waiting for? Let's go!' he shouted. The four of them took off along the garages as the zombies spilled from the window like lemmings over the top of a cliff.

They leapt across onto another set of garages. The pursuing zombies didn't seem to have the brains to make the jump and just tumbled into the gap.

Guy was first to make it to the end of the row of garages. He stopped and helped the others down before jumping down himself. Up ahead, there was a little bridge that crossed the river and led out of the town centre. With the zombies congregated in the shopping area, it was clear on the far side of the river.

The group sprinted for the bridge as the horde slobbered after them. A couple of stray zombies lurched at them from around a corner, but Guy dodged their lunges and pushed one into a wheelie bin. He squared up to the other and raised his fists like a boxer, but Sunny and Ralph clattered into it using the rugby tackles JC had taught them and sent it sprawling on the ground. Guy pushed another bin on it and they sprinted off again as the mass of zombies behind them drew closer.

The zombies were still closing in when they reached the end of the road and clattered across the bridge.

'We need to block the bridge,' Ralph panted, his lungs burning from the run.

'How can we?' said Sunny. 'It's impossible.'

'Leave it to me,' grinned Guy. He ran down the road to a building site and climbed into the cabin of a bulldozer. Its work crew must have abandoned it there.

'Is he stealing that bulldozer?' said Benjamin, his mouth hanging open in shock. He didn't know whether he was more horrified at the thought of committing a crime or the mass of slobbering zombies.

Guy was doing something with a piece of metal he'd picked up on the site, and within seconds he had the machine moving.

'That thing is the slowest getaway car I've ever seen,' said Ralph as it came crawling up the road towards them. 'We'll never outpace the zombies in that!'

But when Guy drew back level with them he didn't stop to pick them up, he just kept going.

'He's doing a runner!' said Benjamin. 'He's going without us!'

'No. Look,' said Sunny. 'He's driving it towards the zombies.'

They watched as Guy, very slowly, charged the bulldozer at the equally slow-moving zombies. He powered onto the narrow bridge just as the zombies reached it at the other end and got halfway across before the tracks ground to a halt and the vehicle wedged itself, stuck fast, in the middle of the bridge. Guy leapt from the cabin and climbed up to the roof before making a rude gesture at the zombies. He turned back to the children, gave them a thumbs up and a grin. As he crouched to leap back down, his feet slid from under him on the slippery metal and he tumbled onto the front of the bulldozer, back towards the zombies. He scrambled to his feet, but grasping hands closed around his ankles and drew him into the crush.

'Do something!' Sunny gasped in horror.

'Do what?' said Ralph, his voice softening to a whisper. 'How can we do anything? They've got him.'

'He's still alive Ralph, we can't just leave him.' Sunny dashed forward, running up to the bridge and climbing up onto the bulldozer.

Ralph froze, rooted to the spot, 'Sunny, no!' he shouted. It was like everything was happening in slow motion.

Sunny clambered over the roof and jumped down to Guy. She kicked out at some lunging zombie hands, but more reached up to take their place. It was useless. As Ralph watched, she seemed to steel herself and then she crouched and dived at Guy using the rugby techniques she'd learned from JC. Her bodyweight was enough to send him tumbling to the side and they both crashed out of the bulldozer, bounced off the bridge, and tumbled into the torrent below.

Ralph and Benjamin dashed forward, but by the time they reached the river, all they could do was watch as the fast-flowing water carried Sunny and Guy into the distance.

9
Road Worriers

The two boys followed the river downstream, looking for a glimpse of Sunny or Guy. They were hoping they'd see them lying on a bank somewhere, but so far they'd found nothing. Ralph had never thought about the course of the river before, but he realised now that it formed the border for the town, separating it from an area of countryside. Ralph and Benjamin were on the countryside bank. It only had a scattering of houses, most of which were close to the bridge. The river curved away from the houses and into an area of fields that made the going much tough. They had to scramble through hedges and over fences and the ground became boggy and wet where the river had previously burst its banks.

Ralph was furious with himself. If it had been the other way around, Sunny would have followed him over the side of the bridge to save him. She would never have hesitated. Just like she hadn't hesitated with Guy. But he wasn't brave like her. He was weak. His parents had always said so and they were right. He'd paused when he should have rushed in to save her, and then in a heartbeat she'd gone.

He stepped into a muddy patch and sank to his knee in the sticky squelching bog. It made a sucking sound as he stepped out of it, and he pulled his leg free to find his trainer was missing from the end. Ralph watched as the mud closed back over the top of his shoe, sealing it into the mire. He tried to hop forward onto a dry patch of land, but his other foot caught and he toppled forward, splatting face-first into the mud. He scrambled out onto the drier patch and glared at Benjamin.

'This was a terrible idea. We can't follow the river this way,' he spat, trying his best to brush the mud from his clothing. 'We should just swim across.'

'That's not a good idea, Ralph. People have drowned in there. Look, there's a lane on the other side of those bushes,' Benjamin nodded towards a bushy hedge that separated the field from a narrow road. 'We'll be able to follow it back to where it joins the main road and then follow that into town.'

They pushed out through the bushes and onto the narrow lane that was sometimes used to run boats down to the river. The lane connected to another road that ran back into town over another bridge that crossed the river further downstream. It was a longer walk to get where they needed to go, but it would be quicker than trying to cut across country.

When they eventually reached the intersection where the lane met with the road, they were tired, hungry and thirsty.

'I need a drink, Ralph. I'm dead on my feet here,' said Benjamin, who collapsed to the floor as if to illustrate his point. 'No pun intended,' he added.

Ralph slumped next to him. 'We're out in the middle of nowhere, we've lost Sunny, we're covered in mud and our cardboard body armour has fallen to bits. Not to mention a horde of zombies have taken over the town. I'd say grabbing a sandwich is the least of our worries right now.'

'Quiet,' shushed Benjamin. Ralph opened his mouth to object, but Benjamin waved him into silence. 'Do you hear that noise?' he whispered.

The boys strained their ears and could make out a distant creaking and what sounded like wailing.

'What is that?' said Benjamin. 'More zombies?'

'Whatever it is, it's coming down the road...'

The creaking grew louder, and the wailing became a chant. 'Warriors! Warriors! Hear our roars! We want more stuff, we'll take yours! Warriors! Warriors! Hear our roars! We want more stuff, we'll take yours!'

Around the bend emerged a group of kids pushing a shopping trolley. There were two boys and a girl. One boy was large and muscular with a head like a slab of granite, the girl was short with dark intelligent eyes, and the other boy was round and flabby. All three wore ripped clothing and had used marker pens to give themselves fearsome 'tattoos' on their arms and faces. The girl was wearing a pair of swimming goggles for no apparent reason.

'Oh no.' Ralph closed his eyes in despair. Just when he thought today couldn't get any worse, his three least favourite people turn up to top things off.

'Do you know these kids?' asked Benjamin.

'I'm afraid I do,' muttered Ralph under his breath. 'They go to my school. Call themselves *the Wrecking Crew*. And it looks like they've gone feral. The big one—that's Breezeblock—rumour is his dad dropped a brick on him when he was a baby, but the brick smashed into pieces on his skull. He's the leader. The little one is Parsnip, she's a mouthy little git and she'll get you into trouble if she can. The round one is Plomp. He's just there for appearances, I think.'

'He doesn't look very decorative,' said Benjamin.

'He's not pretty, but he adds a certain heavyweight menace I suppose,' explained Ralph. 'It's what you want if you're trying to be intimidating around other kids.'

The Wrecking Crew caught sight of Ralph and Benjamin, and let out whoops of excitement. They quickened their pace until they drew alongside the pair.

'Well, well, well. Fancy seeing you here, Cribbens,' said Breezeblock.

'Who's your little friend, Cribbens? Not seen him around before.' questioned Parsnip.

She sounded polite but Ralph was weary, they liked to keep you feeling nervous. 'This is Benjamin.'

Parsnip eyed Benjamin with a smirk.

'I like your jacket, Benjamin. I've always wanted one of those.'

Plomp sniggered, but Breezeblock just stared unblinking at Benjamin.

'She likes your jacket,' he said. 'Why don't you give it to her? As a present. She'd like that.'

Parsnip nodded. 'I would. That would be sooo kind of you Benjamin,' she smiled, but her grin was full of menace.

Benjamin refused to back down. 'I'm not giving it to you! My dad's a judge! You won't get away with this.'

'Get away with what?' said Breezeblock. 'We just thought it would be a nice gesture if you gave a girl your jacket. But if you don't want to, then fine. And by the way... your daddy might have been a judge yesterday, but since all them ghouls appeared, everything's changed 'round here. There's no law.' Breezeblock took a long pull on a can of energy drink that he'd whipped out of the shopping trolley. 'This is the wild west!' he jeered.

Parsnip sniggered, and Plomp gave a loud guffaw. Ralph laughed along, and Benjamin just stared with a horrified look on his face.

'Well it's been lovely to see you Breezeblock,' said Ralph with a cheery nod of his head. 'And we hope everything goes well with your post-apocalyptic road gang, but we must be on our way, we're meeting Sunny, you see and—'

Parsnip let out a burst of sputtering laughter.

'Pfft, don't think so, Cribbens. We saw your little girlfriend being pulled out of the river. You should just join up with us now. We're heading cross-country, gonna live off the land.'

'You mean you're going to help yourselves to whatever you can find in people's empty houses. What do you mean you saw Sunny being pulled from the river? You mean Guy pulled her out?'

'No idea who Guy is, but a bunch of ghouls pulled her out over in the town. Soo, like I say, join up with us. We've got a few tattoos left and you can bring your friend too.'

It was then that Ralph noticed the chiffon scarf that Parsnip had around her neck. It was the scarf that Sunny had been wearing, with little giraffes sewn into it.

Ralph felt his blood run cold and a desperate rage filled him. He'd had enough of being pushed around by these idiots. This was the final straw. This time he wouldn't let them make fun of him or his friends without a fight.

118

Screwing his face up, he launched himself at Parsnip, grabbing for the scarf and sending them both sprawling to the ground.

'Oy what are you doing? You can't do that to a lady!' said Breezeblock as Benjamin made a feeble attempt to pull Ralph back. Ralph though, had lost control and grabbed out at Breezeblock's ankles, pulling him down into the brawl.

Ralph growled like a wild animal and threw all his energy into grappling with Breezeblock. Breezeblock though, was the size of a full-grown man and built like a wrestler. He stood up easily, pulling Ralph up with him, before shoving Ralph back to the floor.

'You're getting big for your boots, Cribbens. Who do you think you are? Messin' with us!'

'Give me that scarf, that's Sunny's scarf!' Ralph shouted.

'Was,' snapped Parsnip. 'If Little Miss Clever Clogs wants it back, she can come and ask me for it herself.'

'You just told me she got grabbed! Give it here!' Ralph lunged at the scarf, but Breezeblock stepped in front of him and shoved him back towards Plomp, who grabbed him from behind in a bearhug.

Parsnip moved in front of Ralph and pushed her head into his face so they were eyeball to eyeball. She rolled her ragged sleeves up. 'You're going to regret that, Cribbens.'

She drew her hand back and jabbed him in the stomach before balling her fist up to strike him again.

The sound of an engine approaching made them all turn and look. None of them had seen any traffic on the roads around town all day.

A white minibus, covered in patches of rust, came sputtering around the corner. Its engine grumbled and complained as it came wheezing up the road before pulling over next to the amazed group who stood staring at it open-mouthed. Only a day ago, cars and trucks had been a huge part of the soundtrack of everyday life, but in the eerie quiet that had crept up on them, the diesel engine of the minibus ripped the air like a drill.

'Alright boys?! What's 'appening 'ere then?' said the large man in the tracksuit through his open window.

'I'm a girl, you buffoon!' snapped Parsnip.

'JC!' said Ralph, with a burst of genuine pleasure at seeing the old rugby coach.

'Alright boy? How's it going?' JC gave each of the kids a quizzical look.

'Where's your little pal gone?'

'She got lost. We think the zombies have got her.'

JC nodded, his face hard. 'She's a fiery one. Reckon she'll be alright. Let me give you a lift home,' he glanced at Breezeblock, Parsnip and Plomp as well as Benjamin. 'You can come too if you want?'

Benjamin jumped straight into the minibus, but Breezeblock shook his head.

'You must be joking,' said Parsnip. 'We're having way too much fun out here.'

JC nodded and looked again at Breezeblock.

'Why don't you come along to training next Saturday, up at the sports pitch?' he said, as if nothing happened. 'You'd make a cracking second row for my rugby team. And your friends would be quite handy as a scrum-half and a prop.'

Breezeblock just chuckled.

120

Ralph got into JC's minibus and the three of them pootled up the road, the old minibus' engine sputtering.

10
How to Stop a Killer Zombie

Ralph allowed JC to drive him back to his house without protest. His plan of finding Sunny had evaporated when he'd seen the scarf on Parsnip. He knew he had no chance of getting to her without getting pulled apart by the zombies and hoped that she and Guy had got away somehow. While he bounced along in the minibus, another plan had come to him. He'd remembered that back in his house he had a comic somewhere that had featured zombies. It had been one of the first he'd read, and he couldn't remember too much about it, but he felt it could hold a clue about what they could do to defeat them and return the people to normal.

It was quiet in the car. Ralph gave JC minimal directions back to his house while Benjamin sat in silence, staring out of the window.

As they made the way through the streets of the sleepy town, things seemed even sleepier than usual. Apart, that is, from the pockets of dead-eyed zombies that milled around the streets.

JC pulled the minivan up on Bushy Lane. 'Do you want us to come in with you, boy?' He said as Ralph hopped down onto the road.

'Nah, it's fine, I shouldn't be long. It's best if you wait here to avoid any awkward questions from Dad.'

Ralph realised with a pang of guilt that he hadn't even thought about Dad and Imelda since he'd set off this morning. He should have been concerned in case something had happened to them, but with everything that had gone on, it had never even occurred to him to worry. Now though, as he opened the front door, his heart started pounding in his chest and his fingers became clammy with sweat. He'd already lost Sunny today and despite his father's and Imelda's numerous flaws, he didn't want to lose them too.

All was quiet as Ralph crept inside. It was only a few hours since he'd set off with Sunny to look for missing pets, but it felt like he'd been away for much longer. The familiar old maroon coloured carpet in the hall looked threadbare. The magnolia paint that covered the walls was yellowing and smudged with dirty finger marks. He'd noticed none of this before, but something inside him had changed and he was seeing everything with a new perspective.

Ralph's dad emerged from the living room. His brown corduroy trousers and his powder blue shirt hung limply from his thin frame. His face was pale, and he looked even more gaunt than usual, but to Ralph's relief his brown eyes were still sharp and human.

'Hullo Ralph,' he said. 'Where've you been all day?'

'I've been out with Sunny,' Ralph replied as if that explained everything he'd been through.

'Right. I don't suppose you've seen your brother, have you? Imelda's been worried sick.'

'Erm... I saw him in town earlier on, but I'm not sure where he is now. He was with some... err... friends...' Ralph replied, thinking back to when he'd spotted Luca at the police station.

'I suppose he'll be alright,' said Dad. 'He's been going out a lot lately. I'm sure he knows his way around by now. If you go back out though, can you keep an eye out for him? Tell him to come home for a bite to eat.'

Dad gave Ralph a weak smile and ducked back into the living room.

Ralph thought Luca must have had enough to eat already. He imagined he'd filled up on human flesh while he was rampaging around the town with his zombie pals.

Dad's mention of food got Ralph's stomach going again, so he popped into the kitchen and got himself a glass of water. He grabbed a loaf of bread and a piece of cheese from the fridge and made up a bottle of lemon squash before putting them in a bag to share with Benjamin.

He hefted the bag over his shoulder and headed upstairs and up the ladder to his penthouse room in the attic.

He flipped the lid on the old sea chest where he kept his precious comics. *There must be something in here*, he thought. Somewhere in the stack of well-thumbed pages there had to be a clue that would tell him how to deal with zombies. He knew he'd read something about it before. If he could find it, then maybe he could put a stop to the zombie apocalypse.

Ralph started digging through the pile of comics. He was always so careful with his most treasured possessions, but today he tossed aside anything that didn't look like it could help. He knew the one he was looking for, but as he sifted the comics around, there was no sign of it.

Where is it? He thought, as the stack of discarded comics grew steadily larger than the pile left inside the chest. He scrabbled through the last of the comics, but it wasn't there. Thinking he must have missed it he reached back for the pile he'd already looked through. As he did so he spotted a corner peeking out from inside the cover of another comic. He tugged it free and out slid an old issue of *Dark Secrets* comic. It had a picture of the hero on the front. He was standing on a tower surrounded by a horde of hideous, slobbering, bloodthirsty zombies that filled the rest of the cover. Ralph felt a thrill of elation. *This was the one! The answer must be here somewhere?*

He flipped open the comic and scanned through. His usual reading style was slow and meticulous, taking in every detail of the words and pictures, but he wasn't reading for pleasure this time, he was reading to save his friend's life - if it wasn't too late already.

The story was a good one. It was about how a warlock had used an ancient amulet to wake the dead, and they'd come crawling from their graves to wreak havoc on the living. Not quite the same as what was happening in Great Merritt - as far as Ralph knew, nobody had returned from the dead - but these zombies infected the living if they scratched or bit them. The hero was a man who hunted monsters and demons. He'd come to the town to help but had run into trouble until an old priest had told him what he needed to do: to stop a zombie, you must destroy the brain or remove the head. Zombies also have an aversion to fire, so you can use that to control them.

This was not good news for Ralph. He couldn't see himself removing somebody's head or destroying their brain. The fire thing might help, but he'd couldn't think how he could use it without burning down half the town and he might not even be able to pick which half.

He slammed the lid on the chest, climbed down the ladder and trudged back downstairs, going straight out through the front door without calling in on Dad in the living room. He needed to talk to Benjamin and JC and see if they had any ideas on how they could use the fire.

He went out of the front gate and found the minibus still parked on the road. Benjamin was snoozing on one of the back seats and JC was standing on the roof, on full alert for any zombie activity. He waved at Ralph as he approached and jumped down to greet him.

'Any luck then, boy?'

Ralph shook his head slowly.

'Not really. I found out that you can stop them by cutting their heads off or destroying their brain or they're also afraid of fire.'

'That's something, isn't it? In fact, the best thing to do is find the one that started all of this. Your brother, wasn't it? Find him and cut his head off. That might make all the others return to normal then.' JC said this in such a calm and measured tone that for a moment Ralph accepted it as a sensible suggestion, but then he snapped to his senses.

'We can't cut Luca's head off!' Ralph said. 'Dad and Imelda would roast me alive! And anyway, that's too horrible to think about. We wouldn't really be able to cut someone's head off we would?!'

JC gave a noncommittal shrug of his shoulders.

In the minibus, Benjamin sat up. 'Why don't we show them internet videos of people playing computer games? My mum always says those things rot your brain!'

'That's not helping Benjamin. Jacob Harvey at school watches those for at least five hours a day and he's still got a brain... well... *technically.*'

Ralph's front door banged open behind them and Imelda Cribbens burst out with Joshua trailing in her wake.

'Imelda, just wait there, dear. You're not yourself, I can tell. You just need to rest until Luca gets back!'

'Ohhh no,' Ralph turned to look over his shoulder.

Imelda lurched towards them with the shambling walk that had become all too familiar. Ralph had seen that walk a hundred times already today. The walk of the brainless zombie. Ralph looked into Imelda's eyes and the cold lack of emotion there confirmed he was right.

'Dad! Get away from her!' he bellowed at his Father, but Joshua's expression darkened. He stopped in his tracks, but Imelda continued to lurch towards Ralph.

'Ralph! How dare you! Can't you see your stepmother is sick? I told you, the worry over you and Luca has made her quite unwell!'

Ralph snorted.

'When has she ever worried about me? When have either of you?'

He pointed an angry finger at his father.

'You couldn't wait to get Luca in to replace me! You think I'm pathetic, that I can't do anything for myself. Well, I can Dad and I've proved that today. I'm not useless, I can do anything I put my mind to. I know that now!'

'Of course you can, Ralph. Imelda and I never doubted it. We wanted another son, yes. But not to replace you. We just thought you needed a bit of help to come out of your shell and, I'll admit, I found you frustrating at times but you're every bit your own man Ralph and we love you all the more for it.'

Joshua glanced at Imelda who stood between them, apparently unsure of which of them to lurch at.

She looked back at Joshua and made her decision. With a turn of speed that Ralph had never seen from one of these zombies, she threw herself towards Joshua, gnashing her teeth.

Before he could think about what he was doing, Ralph was in motion and diving at his dad. Joshua had moved towards his wife, thinking she was coming to give him a hug. Ralph dipped his shoulder and, catching his father around the waist in a tight arm lock, drove him to the ground away from the outstretched arms of Imelda. They hit the ground hard, and Ralph could hear the air exit his dad's lungs with an audible *oof!*

'Cracking tackle that boy!' he heard JC say with pride, but he had only a moment to take it in before Benjamin followed up with a shout.

'Lookout Ralph!'

Imelda was standing over them, her eyes burning with fury. They'd whipped her lunch away at the last second and she wasn't happy about it.

Joshua tried to stand, but Ralph pulled him back to the ground.

'She's not herself anymore, Dad. She's a zombie.'

his dad looked bemused, but he didn't react or fight back against Ralph. It must have been dawning on him that something wasn't quite right.

She came at them, heavy footsteps thudding along the pavement, and the two of them scrambled back against a car. She loomed over them, her mouth twisted into a snarl of pure hunger and her ice-blue eyes filled with a cold malice.

This is it, thought Ralph. *This is how I die. Eaten to death by my own mother.*

He could see JC and Benjamin running at them, but they were too far away, they'd never get to him and Dad before Imelda's teeth were sinking into them and even just a scratch would turn them into zombies.

She leaned in, her white teeth flashing as she opened her pink lipsticked mouth. A mouth that, as it hung open, suddenly filled with tiny green balls.

What the—, thought Ralph.

'Are those… peas?' he said to his dad, too confused to still be afraid.

'That's correct Ralphie,' said a voice behind him. 'Sweet, juicy peas. They've just become my favourite vegetable.'

He spun to find Sunny standing there with Guy and a smug expression on her face.

'And those delicious, fresh peas are our ticket to a zombie free town,' she swaggered over to him, a homemade slingshot dangling from her wrist 'Did you miss me, Ralphie?' she added.

'I err—' Ralph sputtered, but Sunny grabbed him in a big hug.

'Of course you did,' she said before turning to Imelda and slapping her on the back. 'Are you OK Mrs Cribbens? I didn't get those peas stuck in your throat, did I?'

Imelda coughed and sputtered and spat peas over Ralph and his dad.

'Oh goodness! I don't know what came over me. One minute I was having a little nap, I'd felt woozy since I'd had my food last night, I tried that new takeaway gumbo place but it didn't sit well. I think the delivery driver caught me with his fingernail too as he was handing it over. Came up in a nasty red mark.' She held up her hand to show an angry red scratch on her wrist.

'You should have listened to me, Imelda!' said Joshua.

'Joshua has never got on well with spicy food,' she said, putting a sympathetic arm around him. 'Anyway, as I was saying, I haven't felt very well since last night, so I had a lie down on the sofa. I drifted off and next thing I know I've got a mouthful of peas and a splitting headache!'

'You went mad, Imelda! Quite mad! You tried to bite us!'

'Eat us,' added Ralph. 'You got turned into a zombie by Luca and tried to eat us.'

'Don't exaggerate, Ralph. Imelda would never try to eat us even if she was quite mad!'

'What's puzzling me though is… what is going on with the peas? Why did she just snap out of it like that?' mused Ralph.

'I dunno Ralph, but it seems like getting some fresh veg into the zombies brings them around,' answered Sunny. 'After me and Guy got away from town, we headed back to my place to get some supplies and Mrs Millbanks from next door ambushed us from behind her greenhouse. I tripped and fell through the door, but as she dived at me with her mouth wide open, Guy tried to grab her and she somehow swallowed a cherry tomato that was ripening on the vine. Next thing I knew, she'd snapped out of it! At first, I thought something in the tomato had done it, but then it occurred to me, what if it's just veg? I mean those things crave meat like it's chocolate ice cream, so maybe veg has some sort of effect on them? Turns out I was dead right. I've tried a few different vegetables, but frozen peas are the best as they spread out like grape-shot. You don't need to be too accurate to give them a mouthful!' she grinned. 'Guy prefers to stab them in the mouth with a cucumber though.'

Ralph looked past Sunny to where the thief was leaning nonchalantly against a postbox, an extra-long cucumber resting over one shoulder.

'Cucumber gives you better control,' he said. 'Lets you get up close and personal. You should try it son,' he gave Ralph an unpleasant wink.

Ralph couldn't quite believe what he was hearing but if they could turn the people of Great Merritt back into humans, they had no choice but to do it. The cucumber thing, though, seemed a bridge too far.

'I'll take the peas please,' he looked at Guy. 'No offence,' he said to the grinning young criminal.

'None taken,' said Guy. 'As long as you take down a few of those shambling numpties I don't give a monkey's.'

11
Dinner of the Dead

Sunny paced in front of the group and gave a loud 'ahem' snapping everyone to attention. They'd relocated to Ralph's dad's garage, where he'd set up an old school chalkboard on one wall. Sunny had drawn a map of the town onto the board with several arrows marking key points and locations. She positioned herself next to it with a bamboo beanpole in one hand and the other resting authoritatively on her hip.

'Okay, listen up, folks. It's time for us to respond to the zombie menace that's stalking our streets. It'll be tough, dangerous work, and some of us might not make it to the other side. If that sounds like too big an ask, then now's the time to leave. There'll be no turning back after this. If anyone thinks this is too tough a challenge, the door is over there,' Sunny pointed towards the garage door with her beanpole and glared at everyone watching.

Benjamin got to his feet, but Ralph grabbed him by his shirt and pulled him back onto the garden bench they were sitting on.

'It's safer to take your chances with the zombies. Trust me,' whispered Ralph.

'Now, as we can see from the map,' Sunny continued, this time swinging her cane around to point at the chalkboard. 'The town centre is situated within the bend in the river, meaning there are limited routes in and out,' she pointed to the roads and bridges that had been indicated on the map. 'I can confirm from personal experience the zombie horde is currently located within this area, but it's only a matter of time before they look elsewhere for something to eat. It is imperative that we cover each of these routes and rendezvous in the centre of town outside the police station. To do this, we'll have to split up and work our way in, making sure we dezombify any targets we meet along the way.'

'Guy and I will be unit Alpha. We'll take the main bridge and follow the one way system along Brook Street. Benjamin and JC, you'll be unit Bravo and go via the South Bridge and find your way along Watermill Road. Ralph, Joshua and Imelda, you go down the High Street. This is likely to have the heaviest zombie presence, but it also gives you excellent cover without the chance of too many surprise attacks.'

'Sounds great! I guess we must be Unit Charlie!' shouted Ralph's dad who was rather getting into the whole thing.

'Affirmative Mr Cribbens. We'll rendezvous in the centre of town outside the police station. Now we've all seen these zombies in action, but me and Guy have had to escape them twice and we can tell you they aren't quick, but they *are relentless*. Once they have you in their sights they will never, *ever*, stop. Not until they have cracked your heads open like a boiled egg and are slurping out your brain… unless…' she hesitated. 'Unless you can get a bit of fruit or veg into their snarling mouth before they get a piece of *you* into it.'

Guy hefted a box of greengrocery onto the table and upended it, sending onions and tomatoes rolling over the floor.

'Ladies and gentlemen,' he said. 'Choose your weapons.'

As they stepped forward to choose the piece of veg that they'd take into battle, Sunny gave them a serious nod. 'Good luck everyone,' she said, before turning and stalking out of the garage with her hands clasped behind her back.

* * *

Ralph scuttled down the high street, ducking behind parked cars and pressing himself against any walls that he could take cover behind. He was wearing a fresh set of egg box armour and wielding his old spud gun, which he kept cocked and loaded at all times. He'd found it in a box of old toys in a corner of his attic penthouse.

Ahead of him his dad wore an old set of cricket pads for protection and he'd armed himself with a sprig of broccoli on the end of a broom handle. Joshua seemed to be enjoying himself. He had a huge grin on his face as if this was a great game.

Imelda was striding down the street on Ralph's left. She'd taken the fact that she'd been zombified as a personal insult and she looked determined to make up for it. For a weapon, she flourished a cabbage that she'd attached to a piece of string, which she twirled menacingly around her head like a mace and chain.

Ralph wondered how it had taken a zombie outbreak for them to come together as a family. *Sometimes only a tragedy can make us appreciate what we have*, he supposed. It occurred to him that perhaps his parents would let him have floorboards in his room after this. He should probably ask while Dad was in a good mood.

'CONTACT!' Joshua bellowed as the first of the zombies staggered from an alleyway.

It was a middle-aged man wearing a Manchester United football shirt. Joshua charged up to it and without hesitation rammed the broccoli into its gaping maw. At once, the zombie dropped to its knees, rubbing at its eyes.

'What the…?' said the man, suddenly very confused about why he was kneeling in the middle of the High Street with a mouthful of raw broccoli.

'I don't understand… what's going on?'

'Nothing to worry about, old boy. You just got temporarily zombified,' said Joshua, giving the man a sympathetic pat on the shoulder. 'You'll be right as rain any minute now.'

While Joshua had been dealing with the first zombie, more had emerged and were surrounding him in a slobbering circle.

'Oh no you don't!' bellowed Imelda.

She spun her cabbage in a great whirling arc before launching it into the faces of the new zombies. Each one fell, spitting out leaves, before blinking and coming back around as their old selves. Imelda pulled Joshua into a hug and gave him a squeeze. Another zombie, a woman with dark hair who might have been pretty a day or two before, loomed up behind them, flecks of drool dripping from her hungry lips.

'Lookout!' Ralph cried, but he was already on autopilot, darting forward and firing the spud gun in one smooth movement.

The potato pellet sped from the barrel, disappearing straight down the zombie's throat. The creature coughed, then fell back before standing up again on shaky legs.

'Oh dear. I seem to have lost my glasses,' said the woman. 'Has anybody seen them?'

She got back down on her knees, searching on the floor for them. Ralph would have offered some assistance, but the zombies were coming thick and fast. Joshua and Imelda had already engaged another trio of zombies and a large group was staggering towards Ralph.

They lost all sense of time, as the three of them poked, shot and bashed their way through what seemed like half the population of Great Merritt. As more people came back to their senses, things gradually got easier. The former zombies cottoned on to what was happening and joined the fight against those who were still hungry for human flesh.

As he took a breather, Ralph realised they'd made their way into the town centre and were standing right outside the police station. He looked around for the others and saw JC come sprinting from somewhere in front of them, tackling a huge zombie wearing a basketball outfit that was lurching towards Ralph. JC and the basketball zombie slammed to the floor, tangled up in each other's limbs. Ralph saw Benjamin emerge from a side street and force a leek into the giant's mouth, turning the basketballer back into nothing more than a rather tall and bemused human.

'You lucky boy!' said JC. 'I'd love a taste of that leek!'

'I think that's the last one,' grinned Benjamin as they surveyed the multitudes of non-threatening people who were surprised to have found themselves milling about in the town centre.

'Not quite.'

Sunny had also made her way to the police station and had her gaze fixed on a gaunt but big-boned figure standing alone at the edge of the road.

'Luca!' shouted Imelda. 'My chubby little boy. Come to Mummy!' She stretched her arms towards him and implored him to come to her.

'He's mine,' said Ralph, gritting his teeth.

Ralph strode towards his adopted brother. He pulled a potato from his pocket and dug out a pellet. He snapped his arm up towards Luca and fired. The first pellet bounced harmlessly off Luca's chin, who reached his cold clammy hands towards Ralph. Ralph scrambled to dig another pellet out of his potato, but Luca was on him. At point blank range Ralph poked the spud gun between Luca's yellow teeth and pulled the trigger, sending the spud directly into Luca's mouth. Ralph fired twice more, making sure Luca got a full portion of potato.

Ralph waited for the transformation to come. Luca chewed the potato for a moment but then lunged towards Ralph, wrapping his arms around him, pulling him close, squeezing the life out of him.

'Brrraiinns!' said Luca.

Ralph's heart pounded in his chest as Luca's serrated teeth brushed against his neck. He braced himself for the end, but then… nothing. Luca relaxed his grip and Ralph wriggled himself free. He took a step back and saw Luca's pale zombie face staring back at him. He loaded the spud gun and fired again and then again, but Luca just stood there, his expression blank.

'Brrraiinns,' he said.

'I don't understand,' said Ralph. 'Why isn't he turning back?'

'Isn't it obvious?' said Sunny. 'Luca is Zombie Zero.'

'Zombie Zero? What's a Zombie Zero?' Ralph asked, scratching his head and looking confused.

'It means he's the first one. The zombie responsible for infecting everyone else. Luca isn't like the others; he caused the outbreak. He never got turned like everyone else, so we won't be able to turn him back.'

JD sighed, 'Looks like we'll have to remove his brain after all.'

'No!' chorused, Sunny and Ralph, along with Dad and Imelda.

Ralph stared at his brother, taking in his cold, dead eyes. From this distance, he could smell Luca's fetid breath too. 'But... what are we going to do with him? He's dangerous.'

Joshua Cribbens stepped forward, 'I'll tell you what we are going to do, Ralph. Luca may be a vicious, flesh-eating zombie but he's also family.' Joshua put an arm around Luca, who just stood there drooling next to him.

'Dad! What are you doing!'

'I've been thinking Ralph that something doesn't quite make sense. Luca lived with us for all of that time, but not once did he murder us in our beds and feast on our flesh. That's got to be more than pure luck, surely?'

'Well I suppose, but—'

Imelda moved over to join her husband and adopted son. 'Dad's right Ralph, Luca could have devoured us whenever he wanted, but he didn't. You even share a room with him, for goodness' sake. What are the chances you could have survived if he wanted to eat you? No, it's obvious what's going on here isn't it?'

'Is it?'

'Yes, silly! Luca knows we're his family, so he doesn't want to eat us. He loves us!'

'That's right,' added Dad. 'Now, for our part, we also have to take some responsibility. We brought him into the country, so we need to be the ones to take care of him. Of course, we didn't know about his cannibalistic tendencies before, but now we do, we'll just need to keep a closer eye on him. Perhaps not let him wander around town on his own where he can get himself into more scrapes.'

'Scrapes! He turned most of the town into undead monstrosities!'

'And you've never done anything wrong, have you, Ralph? It's time for everyone to forgive and forget. We've all made mistakes, but now is the time to put things right. Why don't we let bygones be bygones and you come and give your brother a hug?'

Ralph looked at the pallid skin of his brother, his sharp jagged teeth and his empty soulless eyes. He wasn't keen to get closer than he was already, but Dad and Imelda had a point. Luca could have eaten them if he'd really wanted to, so perhaps they were right. He looked at his parents hugging their adopted son and thought that they'd never been quite so happy as they had since Luca had arrived. If all of them could be a proper family this time around, maybe it wouldn't be so bad.

'Go on,' said Sunny, ushering him towards his family with a big smile on her face. 'It's fine, if he gives you a nip I'll just ping a few peas at you and you'll be right as rain in five minutes.'

Ralph threw up his hands. 'Fine!' He knew he was beaten so he might as well go along with it. 'Sorry Luca,' he said, 'sorry brother.'

'Brrr-other!' said Luca.

'Ahh, we're a happy family at last!' said a joyful Imelda. 'And do you know what? I'm feeling very hungry suddenly. All back to my house for a lovely vegetable soup!'

She found a shopping basket and gathered the veg that littered the surrounding floor.

'I don't think anyone would want to eat anything else right now!' Joshua joined in.

'I don't know, I think I'd manage a cold beer before they put me back in clink,' said Guy, who still had his cucumber slung over his shoulder.

'And I'm going to have to give it a miss,' said a beaming Benjamin. 'Mum and Dad are over there, so I'd better take them home.'

'Bring them with you!' called Imelda as Benjamin ran to his parents, who bundled him up in a hug. 'The more the merrier.'

'What about you, Luca? What would you like to eat?' Ralph asked his brother.

Luca's black eyes flitted towards Ralph, but his face remained expressionless.

'Brrraiinns!' said Luca. To the horror of the group, he reached into his trouser pocket and pulled out a gerbil that was looking very much the worse for wear.

'Oh dear!' said Joshua snatching at the gerbil with a nervous laugh, 'it looks like Luca has a few table manners to learn yet but I'm sure he'll get there in the end!'

28 Minutes Later

'Looks like the ghouls have disappeared,' said Breezeblock sadly. 'Everyone's gone back to normal.'

He was sitting on the hill overlooking Great Merritt with Parsnip and Plomp and watching as a stream of cars snaked their way out of the town centre.

'Shame,' agreed Parsnip. 'Still, it was good while it lasted.'

Breezeblock nodded. 'Most fun we've had in ages. All good things come to an end, I suppose.'

Plomp got to his feet.

'I'm starvin' now, anyway. Gonna go home and get me Mum to knock me up some grub.'

'You're always starving, Plomp,' said Parsnip.

'He's got a point this time though,' said Breezeblock. 'Not had anything to eat all day.'

Plomp rubbed absently at a scratch he'd picked up on his arm. He wasn't sure where he got it, but at one point they'd all jumped into the shopping trolley and slalomed down the High Street, swerving in and out of ghouls that would lunge at them as they'd whizzed past. It had been so funny watching them fall on their stupid faces… except for one time when they'd had a bit of a close call.

One ghoul had grabbed at Plomp's arm. It didn't quite get hold of him, but he remembered now that he'd felt a sharp scratch. It was nothing really, but perhaps they'd had dirty fingernails. He'd get Mum to pop a spot of cold cream on it when he got home, so no bother.

'Yeah,' he said. 'Funny thing is, I've got a real craving for something meaty. You know me, I'll eat anything normally, but right now I fancy some ham or a fat juicy steak.'

'Oooh, yeah. Steak and kidney pie would go down a treat now!' said Parsnip.

'Mmm.' Plomp licked his lips.

'Burger for me,' said Breezeblock, 'we should call in the chippy on the way home. Wonder if they're open again yet. What would you get from there, Plomp? Fish and chips?'

'Brrraiinns,' said Plomp, he had a dreamy, faraway look in his eyes.

'You what, mate? I thought you always had fish and chips? With a battered sausage on the side?'

'What? Oh yeah. I'd have that,' Plomp's stomach rumbled, and he caught himself glancing down at Parsnip's leg where it dangled from the bottom of her shorts as she sat on the bench. For some reason, the sight of it was really making his mouth water...

The End

Printed in Great Britain
by Amazon